"You say, good fortune used to meet you at every corner. But the fortunate person is the one who gives themselves good fortune. And good fortunes are a well-tuned soul, good impulses and good actions"

- Marcus Aurelias

Actors

(Protagonist or Antagonists the reader to decide)

Me – Shruti

Consultant Guy – Paul Jones

Ex –Partner – Sanjay, Sanju aka, Aslam (or whatever)

Ex –husband – Kamal

GP – Dr Randhawa

Contents

1: That was ME Then! 6
2: Roller Coaster rides 9
3: Ex-husband and partner showdowns! 33
4: Being Stalked 47
5: Further Tales of Woes 48
6: Starting a New Job 52
7: Train Buddies 56
8: Fallouts - Relationship untenable 58
9: Waking up to Reality 68
10: Workplace Shenanigans 72
11: Sanju truth revealed 80
13: An Unexpected Meeting – the mask slips 113
14: Lover's Love Lost - Making Sense 119
15: Relationship (leading) to nowhere 121
16: Me a willing Prey– How So? 125
17: Enter Paul NHS Consultant 128
15: Spiritual & Intellectual Minefields teachings 134

1: THAT WAS ME THEN!

Perceived as good looking, highly intelligent, full of wisdom and ability to connect with people, I did not have an enemy. Even if I did, I would not know what they looked like. This intense feeling of loving and caring was towards all who crossed my path, ready to help, support them.

I loved life. I had this buzz about being alive, so full of life, positive, get up and go type. Even when I was down, I would get up, brush off the dirt, and carry on as normal. Such was the purity of my thoughts and my beliefs. I was full of laughter, cracking jokes, making others laugh and as some used to say, 'bringing sunshine into their life'. Another trait of mine was I was always smiling. Nothing or no one was daunting enough to take that smile off my face. On a serious note, when life required, I responded by giving it my best shot. The joys life presented along with its challenges were equally welcome. I took each day as it came and did my best not only for myself, my family, friends and relatives, but all I came across.

I remember, life was so good to me! I worked hard. My job was tough, requiring a great deal of responsibility and involved travelling across the country. My positive outlook on life made me easily approachable, able to motivate others, communicating effectively and having the ability to connect and complete required tasks/actions. At work, I used to do a lot of floor walking to meet and introduce myself and get to know others including their areas of responsibility. This exercise provided valuable intelligence around constraints within the organisation especially when problems occurred. I was able to change my approach towards finding a suitable resolution.

As a single parent with two children, my employment status varied considerably from being self-employed then working as a Call Centre Assistant, later employed as a Business Consultant with Small to Medium Sized Enterprises (SMEs). Gradually making my way to working for an organisation classed as number two in the world. Having started on the bottom rung of organisational structure, I worked and studied hard, gaining proficiency about the organisation's business, systems and practices that soon saw me climbing up the corporate ladder to achieving senior management status. This achievement brought with it a welcome financial boost.

The secret of my success lay in my determination to provide the best for my family, regardless of the type of work I did. It was the dedication with which I carried out my role, making learning of new skills part and parcel of my transcendence. I struggled to understand when those around me bemoaned Monday mornings or heralded the approaching weekend break.

Another point worthy of mentioning is once I left home in the morning, I would leave all my problems behind. At work, my time and loyalty were dedicated to the organisation hiring me.

During my time at work, I quickly learnt about the 80/20 Pareto principle, i.e., what others took 80% of time doing, I could accomplish it in 20% of the time. Planning before doing was another strategy used to map out the requirement(s). I know you're thinking you can't plan for every eventuality; however, clarity of thought & thinking placed me at an advantage over others who did no such thing. Above is an indication of my work ethics, what about my personal life? How did I conduct myself?

Unfortunately, being a single parent, I was no stranger to social stigmas and taboos. Unbeknownst to me, my extended family believed I had let them down by dragging the family name into disrepute and societal shame. When my ex-husband failed to keep up with the mortgage payments that was part of the divorce agreement, and my home was repossessed, that was seen as punishment for my actions (divorce). Even though I was made homeless with my two young sons, not one member of my exceptionally large extended family came forward to offer any consolation or assistance. My (our) so called friends quickly disappeared into a black hole. I became fair game for gossiping and maligned behaviours suddenly existing on a parallel universe.

Thanks to Tony Robbins, the Personal Development Guru, I soon learnt that it is pointless talking about your problems because as he says, 50% of the people are not even listening or interested and the remaining 50% are glad you have them. This was my light bulb moment to take responsibility for myself and my sons, to not go cap in hand to the family. Thus, doing whatever jobs I could find to support them.

I am not asking for the sympathy vote; I just wanted to give you a brief background of my life and character. To show you how, despite being determined, hardworking, positive, loving, and caring person, I succumbed to the harsh realities of my life. I failed not because I gave up, I failed because my sons were targeted by members of my extended family and ex-husband doing everything possible to destabilise them to cause problems in my life. My family was being pulled under by malicious talk behind my back and betrayal of my trust. One cannot imagine the number of times; I had to sit them down after a hard day's work to quell their fears and reassure them of my unconditional love for both.

Sounds familiar! Now let's fast forward 30 years!

2: ROLLER COASTER RIDES

It was late Sunday afternoon. A day off for some but it makes no difference to me because I am unemployed. Every day is a Sunday for me.

I entered the underground parking area of the Longridge car park. I was driving straight when suddenly this car, drives out from within parked cars and nearly crashes into me. I braked hard to avoid the car and stopped dead. This guy gets out and profusely apologises offering to pay for damage or exchange details. Since no harm was done, there was no need. I accepted his apology and drove off to find a parking place muttering to myself, what an idiotic moron- taking a short cut through parked cars like that!

Having parked my car, I went into M&S to browse their latest range of clothes feeling happy that I managed to find a couple of items. Having paid for them, I made my way down one floor. As I stepped off the escalator, I heard someone say, "Hello, nice to bump into you again." I did not pay any attention as I assumed it was someone trying to attract another's attention, so I continued walking. Then I heard a man's voice saying, 'Are you still angry with me?" I turned around and it was the guy who nearly crashed into my car earlier. I smiled at him and asked what he was purchasing to which he replied nothing yet because I am struggling to decide. I looked around and realised that I was in the menswear department. I looked at him and asked what items he was interested in, and he replied that he needed to purchase a suit for a wedding. Flippantly, I asked if it was his wedding? He smiled as he explained it was not his wedding but one of his close relatives'.

This was the first time I noticed that he was tall, dark and handsome looking person with a beautiful smile that made me smile back at him. I found myself going around the suits area helping him choose something and before long we were joined by a sales assistant who assumed we were together and was bemused when I told him we weren't. When this guy went to try on a suit, I told the assistant how and where we met. He burst out laughing saying it was meant to be, me helping him choose an outfit for the wedding. Choosing the outfit was the problem because I did not know the guy, though I could visualise him wearing some of the gear selected. Annoyingly, the shop assistant kept showing him different items. It was becoming a tug-of-war but somehow the guy was more inclined towards my choice and before long he was heading towards the checkout having chosen items of clothing for the wedding he was attending.

As I was walking away from him, he called out and asked, "How about I treat you to a coffee as a thank you for helping me out? Please!" How could I refuse this handsome hunk, thus agreeing to meet him in the M&S café as I wanted to purchase some coffee mugs as well.

Having purchased the mugs, I made my way to the café area and as I entered it, I saw him waving me over. I went to where Paul was seated, and he stood up as I got to the table and asked what I would like to eat or drink. I asked for a pot of tea with extra milk and sat down as he made his way towards the counter leaving the suit carrier and another shopping bag.

As Paul and I were seated by the window, I found myself staring out and reminiscing about my ex-partner who I used to love shopping for, selecting most of his clothes, shirts, ties, shoes etc. Many a times, I had helped him match a tie with a new shirt and it always used to surprise him to see my choice as not something he would select and yet it was different and chic. Just thinking about him made me sad it was as if I wished he was here with me now. If only I could see him one more time. Tears came streaming down my cheeks and I breathed a heavy sigh thinking of the terrible way we parted company.

He was not meant to be, but the wounds are still raw, and I miss him so much. Trip down memory lane is fraught with a deep sense of loss, like a bereavement. I keep pushing memories to the back of my mind and have not been able to speak to friends or family about the emotional roller coaster I was on. He was the love of my life; we were meant for each other, my soul mate. I was madly in love with him and then having to wake up from my dream-like existence to discover it was all one sided. All the signs were there but I chose to ignore them repeatedly, paying a heavy price for allowing my heart to rule my head. I was known for being a practical, level-headed person, not known to get carried away but alas, falling for him changed all that.

I was wondering where he was and what he was up to if he too missed me. My thoughts were interrupted by the sound of a tray being put on the table. I looked up quickly wiping my eyes and turned around to face my 'accident- encounter' guy. He looked at me asking if I was, ok? He joked that he had only been gone ten minutes, and it looked like I was already missing him! He smiled and so did I. I felt like bursting out crying but there was something about his smile that brought me back to the present moment and I was grateful for that.

He settled down sipping his latte pushing a slice of carrot cake towards me. How did he know I loved carrot cakes? I said thank you, picked up a fork and started to eat stopping suddenly when I realised that I was sitting in front of a stranger eating cake he just brought for me, and I did not even know his name!! How ridiculous or selfish of me.

I put my fork down and introduced myself," My name is Shruti. Nice to meet you and thank you for the coffee and cake."

He put his hand out introducing himself saying it was a pleasure and that his name was Paul. He said he was grateful for my patience in helping him choose his clothes and that it was a weight off his mind because even though he came shopping to buy items for the wedding, he did not have the inclination or the knowledge of what to get. The last time he did any shopping his sister accompanied him. I looked up thinking liar! How can a good-looking guy like him be single? It is as if he had read my mind interrupting my thoughts by saying that he was single and been divorced for over ten years. Pull a fast one, I thought. I do not believe you!

The handsome, gorgeous, guy repeated his name was Paul Jones and I am an Oncology Consultant at the University Hospital Birmingham and as you already know I have an invitation to a family wedding. I cannot thank you enough for all that you have done for me today. I apologise for the near accident and causing you any annoyance. I reiterated that I was not annoyed and no need to apologise curiously wanting to know more about the family wedding. Silly me, it was as if I was expecting an invitation. "Who is getting married", I asked?

"My cousin's daughter. We are a close-knit family, so I am looking forward to attending the various celebrations and functions. The wedding ceremony is next Saturday, and the stag do is this Friday."

"Going anywhere special for the stag do?" I asked.

"Yes! We are going to Amsterdam," he replied.

I rolled my eyes at the mention of Amsterdam, and he noticed saying it's a family outing and no, we are not going to the red-light areas!

We both burst out laughing.

We continued chatting until I noticed the time and told him that it was getting late, and I needed to be somewhere else. I thanked him for the coffee, picked up my bags and started to leave.

I heard him call out, "Wait a bit! I too am leaving."

Paul and I walked to the carpark together and I pointed out where my car was parked. He said it was nice meeting me and leaned over to kiss me on the cheek, taking me by surprise. As he was walking away, he called out thanking me for my help. I waved to him, and he waved back.

As I opened my car door, I thought to myself, what a strange but pleasant experience. This meeting was not planned, yet happened and we have parted company, both of us happy without exchanging contact details or expecting to meet again. Damn!! As I drove out of the car park, I looked into my mirror and noticed a beaming smile on my face. Driving back home, however, my head soon filled with mundane day to day stuff including getting back home and cooking.

I walked in and was met with the usual." Hello Mum, how was your shopping trip? Are you cooking or do you want me to?"

"No son "I replied, "I will cook tonight".

I left my shopping downstairs and went up to change before making my way into the kitchen. Whilst cooking thoughts of my encounter earlier with Paul came to my mind. I shook my head and laughed, sort of missing him.

After that day, life continued as normal except for the times I found myself thinking about my ex-partner, Sanjay. Sanju was my pet name for him. I was missing him like crazy. I had heard many times that time is a big healer. Not for me. It seems no matter what I am doing or where I am, Sanju is always around. At times I find myself looking around to see if he was here.

My favourite song at that time was by the group Foreigners: '*I want to know what love is and I want you to show me*'.

It is as if it had been written for me, desperate to love and be loved. My life was full of sadness, loneliness, emotionally charged feeling, sensing abandonment.

Sanju, my ex-partner, and me we were so close, people used to comment that we looked so much alike, always full of fun and used to make each other laugh. We had so much in common especially our interest in business and money-making ideas.

When I met Sanju, he was single, came across as being attractive, had an air of elegance and grace about him as well as being tall, dark features and had a saunter when walking. Sanju was quietly spoken, beautiful broad smile and well mannered.

As well as working part-time in a Post Office, I owned a frozen food stall in the 'Inshops' indoor market that was open for three days a week. I was also going through a divorce and facing an uphill struggling due to problems with my extended family who held me responsible for the break-up. With two young children, working part time, running a market stall, and going through the divorce procedures, I was in the thick of it, totally immersed in my life's dramas or trauma.

Sanju, used to help-out his brother-in-law with his menswear market stall and was based elsewhere so only quickly visited now and then. Apart from the usual formality of saying "Good Morning or Good Night", I never did talk to him.

After a few months, Sanju opened a Ladies stall in the same market, and we started talking a bit more and before long we started ordering our lunch together and chattering increasingly. I remember one day when I went over to say Goodbye to him as I was doing an afternoon shift at the Post Office, he said to me, "I will miss you" and I showed him a chewing gum wrapper I had written earlier, "Miss you too". Wow! That was something special and I do not remember what prompted me to write that, but I did.

After that day, I realised that I was attracted to him and he to me. We started meeting outside when the market was closed and after work at the Post Office. Soon, I was on cloud cuckoo land as he made me feel special calling me his princess and repeatedly telling me I was beautiful and that he loved me. This was something my soon to be ex-husband had never said.

I had fallen for Sanju completely and there was nothing I would not do for him and him for me. For a time, all was well and then as my divorce ended, Sanju, one day suggested we go into business partnership and during the next few weeks we discussed what was involved without any shadow of doubt there would be investments required from me and other sources such as the banks.

Despite my messy divorce and alienation from extended family and relatives, financially I was sound. I was working part time and had a market stall that was doing well. My divorce settlement did not bring any financial benefits. As part of the settlement the agreement reached was that my ex-husband, Kamal, would keep up with the mortgage payments and not ask for sale of the property until our youngest had completed full time education or turned 18. For my part I was responsible for the upkeep, maintenance of our home and providing for my sons. Tell you the truth, I never did think things through or have anyone to talk to. I was reliant on my solicitor's advice. Other distractions such as interference from family members and so-called friends deserting us did not help. I realised that our so-called family friends before the divorce were aligned to my husband leaving me even more isolated and jumped ship at the same time, due to the stigma attached to divorce at the time, my own family and relatives were appalled at the shame I had brought upon them and our community. Even though they knew fully well that it was Kamal who was at fault they closed ranks around him and welcomed him into the family fold because I had refused to have him back when he 'apparently' realised he had made a mistake and wanted things to go back to normal. I saw through him, how he was struggling to cope and realised he had made a mistake my insisting on emigrating to India. I did not believe or trust him anymore. After all he would uproot us all to fulfil his own selfish motives.

When Kamal was given an ultimatum to choose between staying in the UK and emigrating to India, he chose the latter knowing fully well that he had made his bed but was not prepared to lie in it when it did not suit him. He did briefly return to India, but it soon proved to be difficult, and he realised the difference of being a visitor and settling there. After his honey-moon period with his millionaire family in India, rivalry with his siblings and stepmother made him realise he had made a mistake and wanted to return to England. Moreover, some members of my extended family were giving him regular feedback about how well I and his children were doing. There was no sign that he was being missed and after years of tensions and arguments in our home, both the children had started to relax and get on with their schooling and looking happier. This was not welcome news for Kamal who was struggling to settle in his new life and was becoming home sick. Though he had burnt his bridges on both sides, his informers, my own siblings, were advising him to return 'home' before it was too late, and I decide to marry Sanju.

Coming back to my relationship with Sanju; we did go into partnership though not legally as he thought that to be an unnecessary cost and time wasting especially since we were both in love with each other and planned to spend the rest of our lives together. Neither did I push much thinking that after all we were an item, and he was getting on well with my sons. Besides, I had been through so much stress prior to my divorce and since I did not have the will power to take on any more battles especially with someone, I was feeling confident about. You see, Sanju was everything Kamal was not, *and so I thought at that time*, and said he loved me daily, telling me I was beautiful, he brought the best out of me, and we had so much in common. Sanju was a breath of fresh air. He was hard working too and besides we were joint business owners though 90% of the investments and liability was mine.

Enter Evelyn - may her soul rest in peace. I met her when she came to the market stall stopping for a chat. During our conversations, I found out she lived close to me so offered her a lift home and we soon became good friends. Evelyn was an elderly lady living on her own in a flat rented from the Baptist Church she attended. I made a point of visiting her often, taking her out and inviting her home. Both the boys loved her, enjoyed chatting to her and the chicken curry she made for them. She spoilt them with the mint and chocolate Vienetta roll she used to bring for them. She soon became a family member and would make her way on the bus to visit us. When I was working on Sunday's she would come over on the bus to get the boys school uniforms ready. I was blessed to have her in my life and was closer to her than my own mother who became even more distant since my divorce. My own mother thought the world of Kamal, my now ex-husband, and missed him not being around!!

Due to my sound financial investments and loans from the bank, our joint business venture went from strength to strength, expanding and growing. My frozen food business had expanded too!

However, due to my on-going health problems, I had to have a hysterectomy operation and meant unable to work for six months. Whilst I was in hospital, a relative informed me that Kamal my ex-husband was back in the country. Kamal decided to visit me in hospital intending to make-up and take care of me. After he left, I developed a fever and became poorly delaying my discharge from hospital. I did come back home and was cared for by Evelyn.

The hospital consultant advised me it would take me six months to fully recover, and that driving was out of the questions for few months. This meant Sanju took overall control of the businesses. Sanju was working seven days a week, so I did not get to see him much. Since Kamals return from India both my sons were uncomfortable wherever he visited. It was as if their loyalty was being evaluated by their father who started to interfere in how the home was being managed and who was visiting. This started to create its own problems especially when I was still recovering. Friction in our home was becoming the norm, and I struggled to keep the peace.

Within a matter of months, I started to experience behavioural problems from both my sons and my eldest son was becoming more withdrawn refusing to speak to me at times. Every time they visited their dad there would be problems in our home. I could not stop them visiting him or him coming to the house because he owned it and before long decided to move in. I did not need this but was helpless to do anything. I came to know that my own family was in favour of his actions and as I mentioned before my own mother and sisters still idolised him. This gave Kamal the upper hand. Due to my delicate health problems, I did not have the strength to argue or cause any upsets in front of the boys.

I felt weak and got tired easily. Kamal was the good guy doing everything for me and the boys, what more could I ask for, forgetting one key fact that he was the one responsible for the turmoil and upheavals caused by the messy divorce. He had gone off to India to start a new life, but it was not the land of milk and honey he had envisioned. He decided to come back and was now all hunky-dory. No problem! At least that was his thinking and that of my family who could not understand my reluctance to forgive him.

Kamal's continued interference started to have a negative impact on my health, with darker clouds slowly swallowing my existence making me depressed. There was no one I could turn to and Evelyn, my elderly friend struggled with the negative environment in my home, no longer feeling the warmth and welcome she had got accustomed to. Finally, one day she came and sat next to me on the bed with tears in her eyes she apologised for dumping me at a time when she clearly knew I needed her but the current situation with Kamal, my ex-husband, being in the house was causing her problems. She got up, kissed me on the cheeks and left the room. I felt even more isolated and trapped.

Sanju, too did not feel welcome anymore and only came when cheques needed signing or in connection with a business matter. I was still house bound so could not arrange to meet him elsewhere and on the one occasion when I tried, driving was difficult and besides, I was not looking a bundle of joy, nor had I made any effort to dress up or wear makeup. My meeting with Sanju was disappointing, my self-esteem was low, I did not feel much like a woman looking bedraggled. I cried most of the time I was with him, that could not have been easy for him seeing me in such a state. Sanju tried his best to console me, but I was inconsolable and due to my health problems and situation at home, I was getting overly sensitive and emotional. I decided to return home sooner than expected feeling let down. Not sure what I was expecting but seeing Sanju struggling to cope with my outbursts did not help. I apologised to him and left. Driving back home, I was distraught as the only person I wanted to be held by and comforted could not. I wished I did not have to return home. I wished I could have gone back with Sanju but could not leave my sons. Talk about the walls closing in from both sides. Besides, I was struggling to understand Sanju's behaviour. I could not understand why he was getting annoyed with me knowing all that I was going through. I was in the thick of things whereas he was free to do as he wanted to and yet he was trying to tell me just how tough things were for him. I was not in a good place to comprehend his suffering. It felt as if he too was slipping away. Whilst driving back home, tears were rolling down my face making it impossible for me to concentrate on the road ahead, so I pulled over and cried a bit more. Then I cried lots more.

What was the point of my life? No one loved me or cared about me? I had dedicated my whole life being nice to so many now there was no one who genuinely loved me or understood my pain and suffering. I decided that I could not cope anymore and neither did I want to live. I was an emotional wreck, crying, wailing, lamenting, feeling devastated.

Suicidal thoughts flooded into my mind; jump off the motorway bridge, run in front of an oncoming car or bus, crash the car into a lamp post or tree. I was in a dark place surrounded by my own demonic, negative, out of control thoughts, thinking and minute by minute any hope of survival or fighting spirit was leaving me. It was as if I could see my soul abandoning me, like a spirit departing out of me casting the death knell, pushing me to end my suffering. Suddenly, my heart started thumping, I could hear its rhythmic beats getting faster, pounding, trying to force its way through my chest. My throat muscles becoming tighter almost choking me. I was struggling to breath, breaking out in hot and cold sweats.

I started banging my head on the steering wheel and turned round to do the same on the side window when I noticed someone standing outside. As if by magic, I was brought back to the here and now, looking up realised it was a police officer knocking on the window. I desperately tried to wipe my eyes, rolled the window down and attempted to look at the officer who enquired if I was all right. I nodded my head. He asked then why I was parked in such an isolated place. I looked around and saw that I was parked in the middle of a dark country lane with my engine running. The officer again asked if I was all right and pointed out the danger of parking in narrow road. I apologised but he was not having any of it and again asked what was going on. I told him that I was upset because I had fallen out with my partner and left home in a huff. He asked if I had been drinking to which I replied that I do not drink. He then asked if I was ok to drive. I said, 'yes officer'. He asked for my home address and told me to move on quickly as it was not safe stopping place adding that he would escort me back to the main road. I resisted by saying that I would make my own way back, but he shook his head. I humbly accepted his offer pulling over the left to allow him to manoeuvre past me to pull in front. Once the officer was in position, he signalled for me to follow him. I followed him to the main road and whilst driving noticed I was cold and shivering. As soon as we turned on to the main road, the officer waved to me to overtake him. I did that. He wanted to make sure I was all right because he followed me for few hundred yards then turned left into another road. I continued driving towards my home feeling much calmer arriving home and letting myself in. No sooner had I walked in, I got a frosty reception from my ex-husband, Kamal, who knew I had been to see Sanju. I was in no mood for an argument as feeling worn down, I checked on the boys, got changed and slipped into bed instantly falling asleep.

I struggled to get out of bed next morning feeling exhausted still from last night's troubles. Kamal knocked on the door and came in with a cup of tea. He told me the boys had left for school. I could not believe that I had not woken up to get them ready for school. Still feeling vulnerable, I burst out crying, almost becoming hysterical waving my hands about. Kamal was shocked to see my behaviours, trying his best to calm me down but I was inconsolable. Kamal left the room returning some ten minutes later to inform me that our GP- Dr Randhawa, was on his way.

Dr Randhawa had been our family doctor for over ten years and was fond of our family. When told about our divorce, he was surprised because he thought we were a happy family. Anyway, when Dr Randhawa came to my bedroom, he asked Kamal to leave. He promptly sat down and asked me what was upsetting me so much. I once again burst out crying saying I did not want to live anymore and that I had had enough of trying to cope. He looked at me and asked if I felt suicidal? I told him that for some time now I was struggling and day-by-day my strength was wavering. I had suicidal thoughts a few times, just wished I did not wake up in the morning. However, last night I contemplated taking my life, but a passing police car pulled over to check saving my life. Dr Randhawa told me that given my current circumstances and what I just told him; I was showing signs of clinical depression needing immediate support from the Mental Health Team. He left the room to talk to Kamal and I heard him on the phone.

Being our family doctor, Dr Randhawa was aware of the divorce, my operation and knew about our struggles and strife's since Kamal decided to settle in India and now return to England. He tried his best not to make any individual comments about my situation apart from saying it was all getting too much for me, and I needed a break. Also, the surgery getting a phone call from Kamal and seeing him in the house must have come as a surprise too.

Dr Randhawa returned, held my hand saying he had great admiration for me and how I had conducted myself since the breakup adding he knew me to be very loving and caring person especially towards my sons. He reminded me that at this moment in time my sons must be feeling lost, helpless, and worst still blaming themselves for my suffering. For their sake, he impressed upon me, I need to seek professional help including counselling. He opened his briefcase shuffled a little and then handed me a small envelop with some tablets instructing me about taking them. He requested me to make an appointment and visit him at the surgery but in the meantime, he will arrange for counselling. As he was leaving, he turned around and gave me a big smile making me want to return his gesture. It was at this point I noticed that I was sitting on the floor in my pyjamas. Seeing me looking embarrassed, he smiled, winked at me and walked out of the door. I took a deep breath, looked around my bedroom, stood up and repeated, 'enough is enough'.

I gathered my stuff, headed for the bathroom, showered, dressed, came out, sat on my bed, and decided to rest awhile and be better prepared for when my sons get back from school.

I fell asleep only to be woken up by the sound of Kamal talking to someone on the phone. I dragged myself off the bed walking to the door to listen in to what he was saying. What I heard filled me with dread. Sounded like he was talking to one of my sisters, updating them about my 'behaviour.' I heard him use words like, she cannot be trusted, she was acting irresponsibly, staying out all night and behaving erratically. He implied that I had been drinking when I do not drink. Just standing there listening to him spew lies about me and knowing rest of my family and other relations will be informed. I wanted to rush out of the room and grab the phone from him but stopped myself thinking now was not the time to do anything. I went back into my room, tidied myself up and came out of the room. Kamal was on the phone pretending it was a personal call. I let him be.

I went downstairs fuming and cursing myself for allowing the situation to carry on thus far, health problems or not, I should never have allowed Kamal back or anywhere near my sons. The problem was what do I now? Having spoken to my solicitor, who confirmed he had no right to be in the house and said we need to go back to court to have him evicted as he was in breach of the divorce settlement agreement, regardless of him thinking that it was still his house. As per the terms of the divorce the house could not be sold until my youngest son was eighteen years old or finished full time education. I was not prepared to go down that route besides it could take months to get a court date.

I grabbed some lunch and sat down to think things through aware of Kamal hovering around the house as if waiting for someone. Then an idea popped into my head, why not call his bluff? I sat there thinking how to go about it. After lunch, I decided to have a short rest before my sons came back from school. I went upstairs to rest but was followed by Kamal who, having been empowered by his phone call with my sister, started ranting and raving at me telling me I was an irresponsible mother and could not be trusted with my sons. Our conversation soon turned into a full-blown shouting match with neither side backing down. He said I thought more of Sanju than my own kids. I suddenly jumped up and said, 'maybe you are right', and I do not belong here but with Sanju'. I told him that he can have the house and the kids, I was leaving!

As I made my way towards my wardrobe to start packing, Kamal ran out of the room. I stood there with a smile thinking I did not think it would be that easy and so soon. You see that was my bluff to threaten to leave him with the kids and walk out to 'enjoy my life with Sanju'. He was not having it. In less than ten minutes, I heard the front door slam, I went to the window and saw him with his suitcase and holdall heading towards his car. He opened his car's back door, threw his bags in, quickly went to the driver's side, jumped in and drove off. That was that!

As I walked away from the window, I looked around and sensed there was a deep sense of stillness in the house. Time stood still. The house stood still. I also stood still stumped by what just happened. Pulling myself together, I fell to my knees and thanked God for helping me. Last night, I was in a very dark place, feeling suicidal, a sense of suffocation, thoroughly depressed, let down by Sanju when all I needed was a hug and re-assurances all would be well. Before our meeting, I was already feeling low, and his indifference pushed me over the edge.

I got more sympathy from the police officer who pulled over to check on me than the short time I was with Sanju. Thanks to the police officer, a miracle happened, at least that is how I viewed it. I was thinking about it as Divine Intervention. From being suicidal to sitting in my own home was unbelievable. Relishing the thoughts of freedom and feeling liberated seems the pendulum had swung from deep depression to a sense of elation, self-control.

Suddenly the doorbell rang followed by loud banging. Before I could get to the door, it was swung open and to my horror two police officers were standing there and behind them two officious looking professionals with Kamal squeezed between them. I enquired, 'what the hell is going on?' and was told to calm down and to take a seat. When I refused, I was told to comply as it was a serious matter.

One of the so-called professionals introduced himself as being a psychiatrist come to assess me with support from a second doctor to do the same adding, whilst pointing to Kamal, serious concerns had been raised about my mental health and well-being. He added that not only had I attacked Kamal, threatened to kill him but could inflict serious harm to myself and the children. No matter how much I protested, all I heard was to sit down and calm down followed by a series of ridiculous questions. Was I still feeling suicidal? How long had I been feeling like this? Had I ever self-harmed? What made me assault Kamal, who did not want to press charges but wanted to get help for me.

It was clear from the outset these professionals had already made up their mind given what Kamal had been feeding them. I was talking but no-one was listening as they seem to want to move on much to my consternation not realising that I had walked into a well laid trap (by Kamal). Who had used my experience from last night and visit from our GP, added his own story about being assaulted and wanting to safeguard me and his children, to leave the house and call Emergency Services who contacted the police to help with the assessment as I was 'reported' as being dangerous.

I was sitting there but might as well have not been there because no one was listening to me. I looked around the room, Kamal had a silly grin on his face, the police officers were standing in a corner with arms folded and both psychiatrists were busy bees talking to each other and filling forms. When their writing and conferring was over, one of them cleared his throat, and said the assessment proved I needed immediate medical intervention as both doctors have concurred.

The outcome of the assessment was final and binding. It was at this point I noticed there was another person in attendance, a Community Practice Nurse (CPN) who had left the room than come back listening attentively and only spoke after the doctors gave their verdict telling me he was going to find a place for me at a Mental

Health Hospital and arrange for an Ambulance. His phone rang and I was informed a bed was available at the local Unit of the Mental Health Hospital not far from where I lived. I was told to pack a bag with essentials and almost in a dream like state went upstairs to do so. When I turned round the CPN was standing behind me to make sure I had no plans to escape or do anything stupid. As if I would! I protested about leaving my sons, not saying good-byes to them. That was of no consequence given, as far as the assessors were concerned, my mental condition. I had been sectioned under the Mental Health Act.

The Ambulance came and I was marched towards it. The doors were open, siren was blaring, and I was ushered into it soon to be ferried away into another realm. I remember looking back and seeing Kamal standing outside the house looking pleased with himself. Unbeknown to me I had walked straight into a well laid trap. I thought I was smart but, in this instance, Kamal outsmarted me. What a fool? How did I not see this coming? Thus, another chapter of my life was written for me.

During my stay in hospital, small snippets of what happened made me realise how my life had been hijacked by Kamal on pretext of looking after his children whilst all the time trying to drive me crazy and commit suicide.

One question that baffled me was why he contacted our GP? Explanation was to have me sectioned under the Mental Health Act. When that failed, he fabricated story about being assaulted and concerns about my mental health. He used my breakdown experience the night before to plan his next move to have me forcibly removed.

Having been sectioned under the Mental Health Act, I found myself locked up in a ward full of other individuals struggling to cope with their emotional issues. Some were sane, and others walking around aimlessly talking to themselves, letting out loud noises or following staff members trying to harass them. As for me, I was handed some anti-depressant tablets and when I refused to take them was warned I would forcibly be given an injection instead. I thought best to comply.

Here I was incarcerated in a ward and got the impression the doors were locked from the outside to stop patients escaping. Not that I was going to try. You see after a day of being in this ward made me realise that I was a 'nobody', a name or number, seen as mentally disturbed. For whatever reasons, staff members either spoke loudly or came across timid depending on who they were addressing. Somehow, I was at the receiving end of the loudish talking and being ordered to take medicine, sit quietly or go to my room to rest. When I asked for my mobile phone and laptop, my request was turned down and told to discuss it with the duty doctor. When the duty doctor came to do his rounds, he was in a hurry asked me a few questions, checked with the nurse about my medication and behaviour. Can you believe it?!

I am in the room, being ignored, talked about, instructions handed with regards to my medication and all the time not even looking at me. Sorry to admit, I did raise my voice asking why I was being ignored.

So much for the NHS motto, 'No Decisions About Me Without Me'!

I was told to calm down and reminded I was not a well person. I asked about my mobile phone and laptop and was rebuffed by the doctor or was he the psychiatrist? Moved on to see his next patient, cannot say to examine but I suppose talk about them to their staff member. I was stunned at what I had just observed, feeling deflated, lonely, and scared. There was no one I could talk to or trust. The ward nurse walked in with some medications, handed them over, passed a glass of water, saw me take them and left without saying a word. I put my head down on the pillow willing myself to cry but there were no tears. I must have dozed off for a good few hours because I was woken by the nurse telling it was time for my supper (dinner), not sure what was said. I dragged myself out of the bed, freshened up and went to the dining room where the meal was served.

Feeling queasy from the effects of the drugs, I picked up a sandwich, some crips and a yogurt and finding an empty place at a table sat down to eat. After the meal, I made myself a hot drink and walked towards the lounge that already had occupants, found an empty space, and sat down on a sofa. Looking up, I saw the television was switched on, but no-one was watching. There were a couple of patients playing pool in a corner. I leaned forward to pick-up the remote with intention of seeing what else was on when suddenly it was wrenched out of my hand. Before me stood a hurly-burly, nasty looking woman who was shouting at the top of her voice demanding to know why I took her remote. I told her politely that it was not hers but belonged to the ward. An argument ensued attracting the attention of ward staff who raced towards the altercation. This woman had become hysterical saying I had hit her hard and sworn at her. I protested, but before I could state my case, I was dragged kicking and screaming out of the lounge towards my room by two strong staff members, thrown onto my bed, my trousers pulled down and jabbed with an injection on my bottom.

I lay there humiliated, not having the guts or strength to get up and venture outside, so spent rest of the evening in my room, in my bed. The medications and injection had turned me into a zombie. I lost the ability to think, reason or cry. Left in a pitiful state with no one to talk to or even think about. These so-called medications and injections were being administered to calm me down, to feel better, to safeguard me and others apparently as I considered to be unsafe, nothing to do with controlling me or rendering me incapable of standing up for myself. You see, I was <u>now</u> at the mercy of the staff who, allegedly, knew what was best for me without giving a thought about asking me.

Having been in the ward for over a week, I was beginning to lose faith as no one seemed to care about me or took time out to talk to me. The visiting doctor was only concerned about asking if I was taking my medication and behaving. By now I learnt to keep my head down, not to disagree or attract unnecessary attention. Left feeling totally trapped and at the mercy of staff members and some patients who were allowed to assist in certain duties in the wards.

One day whilst staring out of the barred windows of the games room, the sun was shining, clear blue skies beckoned me to venture outside. Feelings of hopelessness, being trapped overwhelmed me, I let out a heaving sigh of disappointment when suddenly I became aware that I was not alone in the room. A familiar voice called out saying 'hello Shruti'. I turned round to see a familiar figure standing before me smiling. I rubbed my eyes to make sure I was not dreaming and immediately tried getting up to greet this person, but my legs were too weak, and I stumbled back down looking forlornly up, letting out a pitiful cry for help. This person came over held their hand out, grasping mine and putting their other hand over mine squeezing it saying, 'hello gorgeous'.

Seeing someone from my previous world, standing there tall as life confused me. I was already suffering through being heavily medicated and confused thinking. Wiping my eyes again, then blinking, I tried saying something, but no words came out. You see no one came to visit me, this was my first visitor, and I was struggling to believe what/who stood before me. I was desperately wanting to show my gratitude to my visitor. Just one person who thought about me, cared enough to want to see me and witness the changes in my demeanour and life. How quickly everything in my life had taken a turn for the worse. This was the person who had re-assured me, told me to be strong and get a grip, saying comforting words when I was at my lowest point in life, through no fault of my own but being too loving and trusting. Innocently, in my life, I had deep-seated desire to help all who crossed my path, so can you imagine the lengths I was prepared to go to help and support my own loved ones be they immediate family or relatives.

No doubt my religious, spiritual, and cultural upbringing played a bigger part. Though there were warning signs, many a times, about others cold hearted, selfish behaviours of others, I chose to continue being nice and inviting them into my life and worst trusting them. Sad to say, currently where most are only concerned about themselves, me and my mind-sets, I had set myself up for failure and heartbreak without realising it. Asking or saying, 'how could they do this and live with themselves', was living or existing on a different plane. Whilst most were living their 'normal', lives, I was on a roller coaster ride between frustration and survival, thinking, imagining something was wrong with me. Never once did it occur to me that I was being deceived, stabbed in the back because some people and good at hiding behind false pretences giving the impression all is well with them. Cloaks and daggers, experts in charades.

Coming back to being in the games room and having to face this person was another example of 'being slapped' in the face. The brief time I had been in hospital, I did not have any visitors or receive any messages. What a shame, in my time of need, this person of all the people I had known throughout my adult life came to be the one to visit. How ridiculous that my yearnings, thoughts were for those who did not care or were responsible for my incarceration. This was the last person, I expected to see before me.

Overcome by a sense of shame and embarrassment, I struggle to look this person in the eyes. Shame because at our last meeting, I had promised to get a hold of my life. Embarrassed, because I was looking dishevelled. Unlike my usual look of being smartly dressed, stylish and made-up. Here I was sitting in joggers and a sweatshirt, no makeup, hair blowed dried but not styled, wearing no perfumes or deodorants. I was feeling yuck!

However, my unexpected visitor pulled up a chair. sitting opposite me, asked me to look up. Reluctantly I did as was asked to do and quietly mouthed 'Hello Dr Randhawa'. He replied, 'hello', but did not ask or say how are you because when I looked up, I could see the shock on his face at seeing me thus. Dr Randhawa, proceeded by asking me to take my time and tell him what happened but before I could reply, he apologised for not coming sooner as he had been away on holidays.

He added that upon his return he saw the correspondence from the Mental Health Authority about me being sectioned under the Mental Health Act. Taking my time, as encouraged to do, I told Dr Randhawa all that happened after his home visit at the request of Kamal.

Dr Randhawa listened attentively, without interrupting me. Me, forgetting, he was my GP, expected a reaction from him, in either his body language or verbal communication. Seeing neither, I paused talking, looking at him thinking, willing him to say something but he listened.

Dr Randhawa cleared his throat proceeding to say that as my GP, it is his duty to check in on me and that whilst he cannot overrule the psychiatric assessment, he has asked for a case review meeting adding there were some fundamental questions that need urgent consideration. Further adding the situation had been out of his hands for immediate intervention until he got all the facts through correspondence with my psychiatrist.

He added he was surprised at the speed with which the situation escalated and felt that some of the initial information given to the MH Authorities had set alarm bells ringing. He assured me that he would do the necessary including ensuring my treatment and personal handling was in line with my human rights. I gathered he was referring to me sharing the horrific incident of being man-handled and given an injection without any prior discussion. I asked him if the way I was managed was allowed and what made the authority behave the way it did?

Dr Randhawa advised that I was well within my rights to ask the staff members the same question but advised, given my current state of health, I may not feel empowered enough. He observed that intimidation by some staff members, patients and lack of support left me feeling fearful and cowering for safety's sake. He said that was not a positive sign of handling someone who was struggling with depression or clinical depression as had been diagnosed by the Mental Health Team. He assured me that he will be talking to the duty doctor.

Rising to his feet, he asked that I look after myself and make sure to eat nutritious foods. He left the room without looking back. The door shut behind him, he was gone. The games room fell silent with only sounds of my breathing. Looking around the games room, it felt different, something has changed since I first walked into it. There was a sense of hope and 'I mattered' resounding, filling the musky air. I stood up, took one last look, walked towards the door, stepped into the corridor, and saw Dr Randhawa talking to someone who was out of my view. I waved to him.

Dr Randhawa was my knight in shining armour, one who brought hope to my despair especially when I was drowning in my sorrows and pitiful state of being. The first thought that came to my mind was that at least someone cared enough to listen to me. He assured me he was going to get some answers whilst at the same time the negative part of my mind warned that he may not be able to move much let alone get me out of here.

Both hope and despair were competing for dominance of my mind. I tried talking positive talk to myself. Reminding myself that all was not lost as Dr Randhawa's visit proved he did care about my health and wellbeing. Once back in my room, lying on the bed, I drifted off daydreaming about Dr Randhawa, my prince charming, in love with me and me with him. I saw us going out for a romantic meal sitting at a table booked for us with floral displays of red roses, a box of chocolates and champagne in an ice bucket. I was elegantly dressed in a long flowing gown made of satin, peach in colour supported by light silver jewellery. I was trying to figure out what type of suitable footwear to accompany my dress when I was startled by a loud voice calling out my name.

"Shruti, follow me". It was a duty nurse standing in front of me, ordering me to immediately follow her.

The immediacy of her voice and order, scared me into thinking that Dr Randhawa's visit had something to do with it. Him sharing the information could have caused an upset or annoyance to staff members. Feeling all sorts of threats, I followed the nurse into a counselling room saying engaged on the door. Feeling very weak at the knees, almost wobbling, I managed to stay upright, entering the room, saw three other occupants already sat sitting in their chairs. I was summoned to sit down. Introductions followed with one being a doctor, a counsellor, a student nurse and the staff nurse who rudely interrupted the only sane moment in my life.

I was informed that the purpose of the meeting was to review my case. Really! That was quick but before I could rejoice, I was told it was a planned meeting. All patients must attend. Planned! Huh! I did not know about it. Cynical you may think but I was thinking how I can be in a planned meeting that came as a surprise to me. I reminded myself that I was in a Mental Health Hospital where I do as I am told. Having been lost in my own thoughts, I missed out on some of the information shared with the group and when I was asked a question, I did not have a clue what to say because I hadn't been listening. Made no difference as the meeting had moved on and it was at that point, I noticed someone sitting in a corner typing away on their laptop, a scribe. I might as well have not been there as notes were read, shared, responded to, but no feedback or input required from me and in less than thirty minutes the meeting was over as the next patient was waiting outside. I was politely asked to leave the room. I was glad to leave as was beginning to feel suffocated and scared at being cornered about my behaviour or some other misdemeanour. What was all that about, I asked myself. Tick box exercise as no contribution or input from me was required.

Walking back to my room, a voice called out my name, it was the office administration staff member holding my laptop bag and mobile phone. I was overjoyed at having them back, now at least I had something of my own to keep me occupied and hopefully, find out what had been going on at home and the world in general in my absence. Getting back to my room, I put both the phone and phone on charge feeling annoyed at having to do that. Sitting back on the small sofa chair in my room, I reflected on the planned meeting, that I was not made aware of, that just took place. Had I been told but forgotten! Could be, not surprised, after all I have not been in control. Others were.

What was all that about? Was I meant to prepare for it? How could I when I wasn't aware it was taking place? Making myself think hard to establish if I said or did anything to cause any upsets. I was there but not. The meeting was conducted for me but without my involvement. What was the purpose or intention? I should get a copy of the minutes of the meeting, think again was I going to ask for a copy and suffer any consequences.

The worst part of this fiasco meeting was having to justify to myself why, how or when I had become a non-person. To be treated so badly, be ignored and talked about in my presence with any thought about my feelings, emotions or respect.

Do they think, believe I am mad? Have I gone beyond a place, where or when I could be pulled back? How do I cope? Am I being deliberately being pushed over the edge to make it easier for them to declare me insane, keep me locked up and forget about me. Why are they being so cruel to me? Do they not realise how scared I am, fearful of saying anything in case I get dragged back into my room and punished. Oh God! Help me! I am feeling terrified of what could happen to me.

The door to my room flung open and a carer emerged telling me it was teatime. I looked at her, forcing myself to smile and asking how she was? She abruptly replied she was well and cutting short any chance of turning it into a conversation, repeated that I need to go get some food. I followed her obediently out of my room, had some food and quickly returned to my room eager to log on to my laptop and check my phone for messages.

Having logged on to my laptop, I struggled to focus and changed over to my phone. There were no personal messages, but a few sales pitched ones that I deleted. Sitting here, I tried to think who I could call and more importantly who would want to talk to me. Thoughts of my children came rushing into my mind and just as I was about call home, I remembered that Kamal, my x-husband, was living there and unsure what he would have told them. Feeling deeply hurt and upset, I decided best not to call anyone since no one had bothered to call me or visit. I knew there were reasons as to why this was happening, but I was too tired to think so decided to call it a day and get an early night. Who knows what battles lay ahead for me tomorrow.

The next day, I woke up early, showered, got changed and went outside to get a hot drink. My ward was quiet with the night staff walking around tidying putting things in place. I shook my head to acknowledge them, and they did same to me. I got a hot drink and went back into my room, lay in bed, and fell asleep.

From this day on wards things started to move quickly as I was once again called into a meeting room where a doctor and nurse were present. Without any explanations, I was informed that I was no longer detained under Section 2 of the Mental Health Act and was going to be released to go home before lunch. The local Home Treatment Team would be taking charge and contact me. I was asked to pack my bags and vacate my room for another patient arriving soon. I did as I was told not having the time to assimilate all the information given to me in such a brief time.

I moved out, my bags were taken to be placed into storage whilst the paperwork and medications were sorted, and I was signed out by the doctor. I went into the lounge and sat there for hours as none of the staff members came looking for me. When I eventually took the courage to venture out to find out, I was told they were waiting for the duty doctor to start his shift. When I enquired when that would be, I was told in a couple of hours he was expected to do his rounds. I was tempted to ask, why the doctor I saw earlier hadn't signed me out but thought best not to. I was discharged in the early evening a taxi was booked for me, a nurse came to the front door with me, handed me my bags and medications and went back into the ward. I got into the taxi and headed for home full of intrepidation.

No prior warnings or arrangements were made for someone, anyone, to collect me and my belongings or ensure I had keys to the house or would be allowed back. I was unexpectedly de-sectioned and bundled out of the hospital the same day. Why? Because they needed my bed. Turfed out and not considered a threat to myself or anyone else. Good to know, I was not part of that decision making.

Arriving back home, letting myself in, I was in no mood to talk to anyone as I heard voices coming from the kitchen area, I took myself upstairs. Had a wash, changed into casual clothes went downstairs and into the kitchen where Kamal, my x-husband and sisters were sat chatting away. Surprisingly, none of them said anything either. Standing at the kitchen door, I turned around, looked my sisters in the eyes and ordered them to leave my home immediately.

From that moment onwards, I put myself on notice to not trust anyone; Sanju, Kamal, my sisters, extended family & relatives, carers, or neighbours. I was determined to get my life back, whatever that was, without wasting anymore time. The only outsider, I contacted was my GP Dr Randhawa asking for help to get off the anti-depressants and thank him for his intervention. No! I was not drawn into any daydreaming as there was too much at stake that required me to be cautious.

Guess what? Whilst, I was in hospital, Kamal, my x-husband, realised that his freedom was hammered having to be around his children and had decided to cut and run. No sooner, had I been discharged and come back home, he packed his bags and moved out. I was sectioned because of the lies he and my sisters fabricated calling me a threat to him, the children, others and likely to harm to myself.

Now that story did not suit his purpose because he wanted to escape responsibility towards his children.

Over the next few weeks, I contemplated suing the Mental Health Authority for the way I had been sectioned and treated in hospital. But after thoughtful consideration, I concluded the NHS was a behemoth organisation too entrenched in its ways, practices, and excuses to warrant wasting my valuable time. I walked away thinking a battle for another day. After all it was my own kith and kin who had let me down and had me incarcerated. I wanted to move forward, knowing there was still so much to take care of, especially the children since Kamal had walked out on them.

The abject cruelty of my own and the Mental Health environment that I found myself in, makes me shudder. To be surrounded by caring staff members who did not care, listen, or involve me their decision-making process. Even when they pretended to listen, nothing of what I had to say was taken on board. According to their own diagnoses of me being clinically depressed, did anyone think how scared or threatening the environment was. I was left feeling worse than when I went in and medicated up to my ears with anti-depressants. No thought whatsoever as to how I would be weaned off them. No! Told, medication was for life. What about helping me adjust back into the real life? Sod you!

3: EX-HUSBAND AND PARTNER SHOWDOWNS!

Kamal, my ex-husband, what happened to him? He moved to London, then up on returning to India married for a second time. Before his move, he had one last trick up his sleeve by not keeping up with mortgage payments as was his part of the divorce settlement. Our house was repossessed, and we (both sons and me), were made homeless and moved into a Council owned property. As if it was not enough to have roof over our heads removed, on that very day Kamal boarded plane back to India and none of my family member turned up to offer us a place to stay.

That was Kamal good-bye.

Enter Sanju.

(Sanju appears on the scene)

Moving onto Sanju and his relationship with me, our business and on a personal level. He explained away not visiting me in hospital saying he did not want to make a bad situation any worse expressing his shock at finding out that no one else did either.

Was his explanation kosher? The truth will unfold later in the story.

No sooner had Kamal left, Sanju started to come over but mostly to discuss to business, by that I mean financial aspects that involved asking for money to either pay bills or buy stock. One day when I told him that I had none, he started shouting and getting angry, saying things like I had it easy whilst he toiled hard to build the business. His angry behaviour and kicking up so much fuss, in the end I went to a bank to withdraw cash from my credit cards. This soon became a frequent practice with him with promise of repaying it back. I found myself applying for new credit cards to keep the business afloat and letting the outstanding balances creep up and up. I hadn't realised Sanju was taking advantage of my lack of clear thinking due to the medications.

I was an easy target he manipulated and used. All the time, due to my financial contributions, I was confident the business was doing well and besides given my responsibilities since the divorce, I felt I had no choice but to keep the business solvent. Sadly though, I was soon proved wrong on the business front because Sanju had been deceiving me. I started receiving county court judgments in the post, in my personal name and worse still creditors came knocking on my door asking for payments. When I confronted Sanju, asking why he had given out my name and home address? His response shocked me when he said why not? After all I was an equal partner in the business.

Once again, my illusion about Indian men protecting their women came crashing down. There was me thinking that it was now *his* responsibility to protect me and the business. Protect he did, but it was his own family exposing me to a series of humiliating situations that I could never have imagined in a million years. I had been blinkered, looking at our relationship through rose-coloured spectacles, blinded by my love for him, failing to realise it was one sided and he was using me. I blamed myself and my circumstances for being naïve. Sanju, had entrenched himself so deeply into me and my family, talking about wanting to take care of us and never letting us down or letting anyone hurt us. He wanted me to keep loving him as no one had done so before and told me he felt valued and wanted. He talked the talk to keep me hooked at the same time fleecing me for every penny he could get out of me in the name of love and our business. Another blind corner was him being in my home most days including after work and at the weekends. But he never spent the night with me citing my young family and respect for me.

As the months rolled by, things deteriorated with Sanju starting to behave aggressively towards me. Mostly, coming over and demanding he be fed, and I sort out the business mess. His aggressive behaviour included slamming doors, throwing things about and once when I refused to let him in, he broke the back window lock, opening and climbing through it. I was standing right there next to the window looking on helplessly whilst he attempted to dismantle the lock from the outside. Most of his aggressive behaviour took place when the kids were at school or playing outside. Soon, every time Sanju visited, I was on tenterhooks or dreading him turning up unexpectedly. Always the thought of my children being around to witness his aggression played on my mind. Sanju was no longer fun to be around, he was negative, full of self-pity.

What impact did this have on me? Increasingly he was eating into my self-confidence leaving me a nervous wreck. Sanju embarked on a sadistic journey of character assassination, belittling me and trying to control my life. Everything was my fault, even him walking in looking upset was my fault. Sadly, a regular cycle of abuse started to take place with him becoming violent towards me, hitting me, pushing me around, shouting and swearing. The more terrified I became, and he could see I was terrified, the more power and control he held over me.

I had never been physically abused in my life. Not by my dad, brothers or any members of my extended family or relatives. This type of abusive behaviour was new to me. Kamal, though selfish, never laid a finger on me, and I was raised in a family where we were all treated with love and respect. Therefore, when the abuse initially happened, it took me by surprise, and I tried to justify his behaviour by thinking I had upset him or wasn't loving enough towards him. He had previously painted a picture of gross neglect by his own mother who left him to live abroad and growing up, how unloved he felt by rest of his family, including his father, he was living with. That was the hook and the trap he used to explain away his bad behaviour or my neglect of him. I was on a mission to convince him of how much I loved him and that I was not like his mother who abandoned him. I was prepared to make sacrifices for him to make him feel special. Sanju had me eating out of his hands using my good, loving, caring nature against him when he did wrong.

Reverse psychology. His mother abandoning and neglecting him was used to make me feel guilty for upsetting him. If I genuinely loved him than how could I hurt him or talk about leaving him. Alarm bells should have being ringing loudly but was I listening?

One Saturday morning, I woke up feeling elated, it was a beautiful morning, the sun was shining and not a cloud in the sky. After showering, I prepared an English breakfast for the boys. I tidied up the kitchen, did some housework and went for a brisk walk to enjoy the beautiful day. Whilst out, my phone rang, and it was Sanju who seemed surprised to hear my chirpy and cheerful voice (his words). He asked if he could come over later and I agreed. Hmmn! That afternoon when he eventually arrived, we went shopping at a local Sainsbury's. He arrived looking glum, a miserable sod for whatever reasons or just maybe on mission to bring me down knowing I was feeling happy!

However, on the way back home and not wanting to take him home looking miserable, I pulled the car over a short distance from home and tried talking to him. I suppose I was being gung-ho as usual. Tony Robbins, personal development guru's positive thinking coming into action. My good intentions and deed backfired miserably because instead of cheering him up, he managed to make me feel miserable and fed up. It was as if I was sitting next to an ogre sapping my positive energy. When we reached home, he pushed past me barging into the lounge, slamming the door after him. *Unfortunately for him and fortunately for me*, both of my children though at home were playing outside with neighbourhood children. This was the turning point in my life. For now!

I felt a surge of anger, fury, well-up inside of me, I took a deep breath, went into the lounge and as I approached the lounge, Sanju picked up a side table with intention of throwing it. No idea what possessed me, but I had enough of his tantrums and aware the children could walk in any moment. I shouted at him to stop his childish behaviour and warned that if he ever threw things at me or around the house, laid a finger on me, slammed any doors or raised his voice including swearing, I would not hesitate to call the police to report him for domestic abuse. Pointing to the phone lying nearby, I reiterated, don't ever push me again. I told him that enough of him abusing me, reminding him that only reason for putting up with it was because I believed it was my fault given my messy divorce and due to suffering health problems. I warned him that I had overly compensated thinking he was being neglected.

I went on to say he was selfish, self-centred and had defrauded thousands of pounds from the business whilst making me believe it was doing well. Further adding that every time I asked to see the paperwork, he either ignored me or called me smarty pants or used some other insulting name-calling to make me back off. When Sanju tried to remonstrate, I shouted, 'enough', no more, stopping him in his tracks. Sanju, sat down stunned because it was the first time, I had ever raised my voice. He had forced my hand when I realised my sons could walk in any moment to witness him abusing me. I had snapped, thinking over my dead body! I was not having that! This was my home, my children and up to me to protect them. I had enough of trying to appease, pacify and cajole this miserable sod.

Sanju promptly got up, rushing past me, closing not slamming the door behind him. He phoned later in the evening to apologise for his behaviour, crying crocodile tears still trying to entice me into his sick, convoluted world. He lamented, as usual, no one tried to understand him, not me or even his own family. This was the hook he had used many a times to pull me into his narcistic ways, to bend to his sickening thoughts and behaviour. Not anymore, not now or ever again was I going to fall for his sentimental, emotional blackmailing, his guilt trips. He knew about my difficulties, circumstances and struggles but it was always about him. His 'poor me' sick mentality and manipulations had debased me, my whole life many a times but no more.

Since my divorce, Sanju's behaviour changed, becoming more demanding of my time and love. Expecting to meet him at the drop of a hat without any consideration of my personal commitments. It was all one sided. He talked the commitment talk but not once took me home to meet his parents or make plans to settle down or keep other promises he made. All he was interested in was money, money and more money any which way I could get hold of it for him, for the business. Sad to admit it but he went as far trying to prostitute me. A bit over the top you may think but no! At his insistence, I contacted an old college friend who was a successful businessperson asking him to loan me some money. We agreed to meet for dinner. The guy confessed that during our college days he was interested in me but did not have the courage to ask me out, though now married with children he was still hoping we could get together at a place he would arrange. Fully aware of his intentions, I did borrow the £3000 pounds from him for an urgent business payment. Consequences of meeting this guy and borrowing money from him were dire as he started calling me late at night, sometimes drunk, flirting on the phone and demanding to meet me. Sanju was made aware of my dilemma but showed little or no interest in helping me. Getting fed-up with this guy's rude behaviour, I would put the phone down on him and decided to pay him a visit at his work address. The guy was shell-shocked to see me on his premises, bundling me into his office, demanded to know what I was doing there. I promised to repay his money and reminded him that I was not interested in being his bit on the side. Suddenly, his wife came into the office, and he had to introduce me saying I was an old college friend's friend. After that visit, he never phoned me, but I did contact him some months later to re-pay his money.

Now you see what I mean by saying Sanju having no qualms about 'prostituting' me to get hands on more moneys. I put myself into the above awkward situation and had to get myself out of it without any support from Sanju. Unfortunately, Sanju had surpassed all limits to feed his addiction about making money and making it big, for me and the children and so he kept telling me. He was stealing money from me and the business.

Moving on, to keep creditors at bay, including the banks, Sanju and I declared ourselves bankrupt, attending court to sign various documents. I was devastated blaming myself for this humiliation and loss of my so-called business empire. Where did all the money go if creditors and banks had not been paid?

To add insult to injury before the bankruptcy, another nightmare situation had occurred that saw me locked up in a prison cell albeit for a few hours. Unbelievable, you are thinking! It is as true as the sun rising and setting on that terrible day. Sharing it here is not easy as it shows another breach of trust and betrayal by Sanju having no concerns for the impact this incident was about to wreck on people's lives. Thinking about that day brings mixed emotions and feelings of ridicule and anger.

I will do my best to tell it as it unfolded.

Whilst managing two indoor market stalls, men's and ladies' wear, Sanju worked the outdoor markets from Friday to Sunday and came indoors late on Mondays. Another stall holder close to me, husband suddenly passed away and she contacted me asking for help in clearing her children's wear stock. Due to traditional funeral practices and ceremonies, she was unable to tend to her stall. She gave me permission for a flash sale of her stock expecting to raise monies to pay towards unexpected funeral costs and to shut the place down.

The following Saturday, I did as instructed and managed to get rid of most of her stock raising approximately £1800 pounds. Later that evening, when Sanju called I excitedly told him about the takings on the children's stall for the lady adding that one of her relatives would be calling round on Monday to collect the money, remove rest of the stock and shut the place down. Feelings of happiness and sadness enveloped me as I was relaying to Sanju. Happiness that I was able to raise the monies for the lady and sadness thinking about her loss and knowing I would miss her as she was a pleasant person, and I enjoyed chatting to her. Overall, I was feeling pleased as punch with myself at being able to help the lady in her hour of need. I placed her sales monies in an envelope, sealing it and making a note of her name and the total. Before leaving for work on Monday, I placed the envelop in my handbag. As usual I went to the market, opened and had Susan, my assistant, looking after one of our stalls. We would swap between us or stand in the middle chatting and serve customers as and when any arrived.

Sanju arrived after midday, went round tiding the stock and then went to get some lunch. Whilst we were having our lunch, the lady's relative arrived to collect the money. I immediately went to get it out of my handbag that was kept in a small unit under the till. When I opened my handbag, the envelop was not there. The usual questions ensued, 'are you sure you did bring it', 'you could have left it at home'. I was one hundred percentage sure; I had checked even when I got in and went to get change for the till the envelop was there, in my handbag. Both, Sanju and Susan scurried round searching both the units for the envelop. This commotion attracted other stall holders and the market manager who offered their help to search the place. All this was happening as the lady's relative waited patiently with a confused look on his face. In the end, I apologised, came clean and told him that I would call him with any updates. He left looking bemused but not before clearing the remaining stock from the children's wear and closing it down.

I decided to call the police who promptly came asking questions about the money. Sanju was asked to go down to the Police Station a few yards away. Sanju did not comeback, but a women police officer came and asked me to accompany her to the station. I was questioned and told that my home would be searched, not his. They took my house keys and left to do the search. In the meantime, I was put in a holding cell. It was late evening before I was released, and my brother and sister-in-law had been contacted to come and fetch me. I was devastated, wished the earth would open and swallow me. When I saw my brother, I became hysterical having been locked up in a cell for a few hours. The first thing he said to me was that I had been set up and no way could I have taken or kept that money. Sanju was standing next to me unemotional and decided to come over to my brother's place. He later went back home to his parents despite me begging him to stay.

The money was never recovered, and the lady phoned me at home apologising for the trouble she had caused me assuring me that she knew me well enough to know that I had not taken the money. Someone had! If the money could not be found, then I was responsible. My name had been smeared. I did not have the means to replace it and Sanju made it clear the business could not either.

It was years later, as my relationship with Sanju turned sour and I discovered he was a prolific liar and defrauded me to the point of using my signature to cash a business cheque requiring dual signatures. This time he blamed the business for what he had to do. The truth struck me like a bolt of thunder when I realised and accepted the fact that it had to be Sanju, who took the money. Yet, I forgave him and continued with our relationship because I was in love with him.

I am not sure whether to shoulder all the blame or to defend myself by saying that had it not been for my hysterectomy, an operation that grounded me for six months, my ex-husband Kamal returning from India, unusual levels of interference from my extended family and relatives that caused conflict and suffering for me and my sons

I had no choice but to let Sanju manage the business, I had to! I am not sure that having signed a partnership contract would have made much difference when it came to being held responsible for loss and liabilities. In the process, I lost my home, my businesses, going from being financially sound to being declared bankrupt, finding myself living off benefits, struggling to survive. Sanju was still on the scene, complaining about his losses and being hard done by 'everyone.' He tried to convince me his losses were far greater than mine.

Lessons learnt! Read further there is more pain and suffering to unfold!

I was in love with Sanju and he with me! Sanju was my first true love not Kamal and at first was everything Kamal was not. When we first fell in love, we were both on cloud cuckoo land, our lives were full of love, laughter, fun and sheer bliss. Sanju was fun to be with, we had so much in common and would talk about anything and everything. He also shared my hobby of betting on the horses especially the Grand National. I remember one year when my youngest son was in hospital having his tonsils removed and we went to visit him on a Saturday when the Grand National was on, we were late leaving the hospital and literally had to make a mad dash to get to the bookies to place our bet. Our horse, Cobalt, lost and we often joked that we ran faster than our horse to place the bet. Whilst at work we worked hard, we made it fun and enjoyed being in each other's company. The only downside was that though we were in business together and in love at the same time, his family only knew about the business not our relationship and his mother once talked to me about Sanju being engaged to a girl abroad.

Was she trying to warn me or had his family become suspicious of our relationship or had a visit from Kamal. You see it was not for me to tell his family, but Sanju who was in no rush to do so. On occasions when his family turned up at the workplace, or the rare occasion, I had to visit him at home, there was a strained atmosphere almost felt like everyone's behaviours was false. I was not welcomed in his house and Sanju would be at pains to avoid me meeting them or be anywhere around his place.

Sanju, had no qualms about driving my car when he did not have one. Sometimes when he was driving and it was time for him to go home, he would drive and park the car round the corner, never outside his home. On the occasions when I was driving and insisted on dropping him outside his home, he would get into a strop with the usual excuse that I get pleasure causing problems at his house, meaning if any member of his family saw us together than he would have a quarrelsome row when he got in. Think about it, he would rather upset me than his family who did sod all for him.

Here again, I missed a vital clue of the lengths Sanju would go to keep me away from his family. I never thought to ask Sanju because I was too much in love with him and did not want to upset him, after all he told me they knew I was a divorcee with children? I felt guilty or was made to think it was because of me he was not parking outside his house. I was not thinking with my head but heart dreaming that one day, soon, we would get married and settle down living happily ever after with his family as my in-laws. Naïve of me to think thus but it brought me such warmth, this feeling of belonging, being accepted and part of his family. The more he tried to keep me away, the more I daydreamt about being happily married. This applied to him wanting me to stay away from his home because any opportunity I got I was parked right outside his house.

Sanju's reasons for keeping me away from his family was due to feeling ashamed of their poor background and low mentality (his words). He said I was smart, intelligent, and had demeanour of princess. His nickname for me was Princess. Thanks to Sanju's critiques about his family, gave me a sense of superiority over them. Once when I was waiting to pick him up, his mother came outside and gave me a mouthful, saying awful, rude, and disgusting things to me. I did not answer back as she came across uncivilised and of a low IQ. She made me feel *cultured, modern, and magnificent!*

Unaware, the wind of change was blowing into other areas of my life.

Things changed after Kamal initially moved out and I started to get involved in the business. I remember one Monday morning when I had been there for five hours and Sanju strolled in, sat down looking grumpy. I tried talking to him, but he was becoming abusive and as I leant over to tap him on the shoulder asking him to calm down, suddenly he lashed out kicking me hard on my shins. It was painful, I was shell shocked and burst out crying. Sanju was apologetic but blamed me for provoking him and profusely tried to show he was full of remorse. He left saying he would bring us some nice lunch to share. I was not myself, felt hurt and scared.

When he returned, I asked to leave, picked my bag, and left. As I made, my way to the car he caught up with me and refused to let me get in. People going about their business were looking to see what was going on. I finally relented and agreed to go for a drive with him. We went to a local park to talk things through and Sanju only let me go home on assurance that everything was fine between us. I knew that if I did not agree with him, he was not going to let me go. This incident was another stark warning of things to come. As usual, I made excuses for his behaviour especially when he became adept at making me feel guilty. There should have been no excuses once he laid a hand on me. I should have finished with him there and then. Easy said than done it seems at this stage of my life I needed him, correction, the business, because I had a young family dependent on me. I had given up my part-time job and invested heavily in the business and was drawing money on a weekly basis for my household expenses.

Unfortunately, Sanju's behaviour became increasingly demanding, asking me to attend Sunday outdoor market in Bristol insisting he needed the stock from the indoor market stalls. I saw it as a business need and before long was committed to going every Sunday. Leaving home at 4 am to reach Bristol by 6 am and not getting back home until after 6 pm. This meant I was effectively working seven days a week. Not conducive given I had a young family to support but I had no choice and besides, I thought it to be the right thing to do and part of being self-employed. However, Sanju's behaviour had not changed once he had me hooked to attending outdoor market on a Sunday. He started to show his true colours, being abusive, shouting in front of staff members, throwing things around including the stock. This was particularly embarrassing for me as he did it in front of his younger brother and two of my Saturday staff who had agreed to work with me outdoors on Sunday. Their incentive being earning extra money and free lunches.

Sanju was like Jekyll and Hyde. He would shout, abuse, throw things around, calm down and then be sweet as pie, apologising for his temper-tantrums blaming the pressure of business and wanting to *succeed for my sake*. But that did not stop him repeating his bad behaviour at closing time again. Once when stock on hangers was passed to him, he threw the whole lot out of the van, and it landed in a puddle. He claimed that it had not been handed to him correctly, this incident left me feeling uncomfortable and embarrassed. He did not care who was around when he created a scene. Younger staff members would get a chuckle out of it after all it was not their stock that landed in a puddle. I was left shell shocked.

Working in the retail sector meant our stock was seasonal with a quick turnaround. Our Men's and women's clothing selection was in fashion, latest styles and colours and replenished on weekly basis. Due to the fast pace of the sales and re-stocking, I was under the impression that we were doing well. Sanju would sometimes ask me to accompany him to the warehouse to re-stock the goods but would not let me go in saying the owner and staff were Asian men who did not treat women respectfully. I was left sitting in the van whilst he did the buying. I felt a sense of pride that he was caring and had my best interest at heart. I failed to realise, at that time, it was a ploy to keep me out late and away from my young family. A cynical person may have seen through this one would think but not me as I was so in love with him and still had blinkers on.

Sanju handled the business finances, paying for the goods and was responsible for the banking. He mostly did cash buying and was given a discount, so he told me. With fast goods turnaround and replenishing, I was feeling relaxed and confident the business had turned a corner after a slow start but also had a niggling feeling with Sanju in charge something could go drastically wrong. It was a deep-seated uneasiness, gut feeling to be watchful. Tales did turn for the worse.

One Christmas Eve, whilst we were doing exceptionally well, and stock was flying off the shelves, I was really excited at how well we were doing and looking forward to having extra cash to splash on my family. At closing time, we locked up the stalls and wishing other stall holders seasonal greeting, headed towards the exit. Just as we were about to leave, two men entered the premises. Both greeted Sanju and said they were surprised he had not turned up as promised thus prompting them to come calling. Sanju was trying his best to usher them out of the premises, but I scuttled after them. Catching up with them, I asked what was going on? One of the men informed me that Sanju had been taking stock and promising to pay them but then failed to turn up. Shocked and annoyed, I asked how much was owed and they said £4,500. These men looked as if they were serious. Looking at Sanju who was still trying to coax them away and pushing me out of the way, shouting at me to stop interrupting and let him handle the situation. I could see there was no handling the situation as the men were seriously demanding their money. I forcibly asked Sanju how much our total takings for the day were putting one of my hands forward. He replied, £5000. I than asked him to tell me the truth about the outstanding amount owing to the guys, he sheepishly replied £4500. I waved my hand in front of him demanding he handover the money which he did, and I handed over the £4500 over but the men complained about being owed a further £500 for some other transactions. One look at Sanju's face convinced me they were right. That amount too was duly handed over. The men hurriedly departed with their money, I looked at Sanju disappointed at what just transpired, shaking my head in annoyance. Without saying a word to him, I walked away from him, depressed and disgusted, got into my car and drove home crying all the way wiping my eyes before I went into my home. In response to my sons asking if I had a good day, I replied that it had exceeded my expectations. I hugged both saying,' let's have a great Christmas', putting behind me the devastating experience at closing time. I was not going to let anyone, not even Sanju, spoil our Christmas. I did not call Sanju during the Christmas or New Year breaks and surprisingly neither did he. Sadly, though, when the children were not around, I would break down in tears fearful of what had happened and what may happen next? A sense of foreboding set in. I wished I had someone to talk to but the sense of shame and having to admit what happened was painful to share or talk about. Again, I was blaming myself and my circumstance.

Around this time, since meeting Sanju, I was beginning to have doubts about the truthfulness of our relationship.

Coming back to what has already been mentioned earlier, by springtime the business went belly-up with both having to declare ourselves bankrupt. This was not an outcome I had expected as I was still holding out that we would be able to manage the situation but there were too many skeletons in the cupboard I was not aware of. I had lost everything including sold my jewellery and valuables to prop the business. Most dreaded were the knocks on my door, open to see Bailiffs standing there demanding to come in and asking for immediate payments of thousands of pounds. Then the phone calls of the same nature. When I challenged Sanju about these dreadful visits and phone calls asking why my contact details had been given, his answer was why not, after all you are an equal partner. Whilst he safeguarded his own family and their property, he had no qualms doing so and there was me thinking it should have been the other way round after all the time, money and support provided to him, nonetheless and not befitting of me to play the victim card. I should have known better. I was too trusting and in love to think otherwise.

Traumatic end to another chapter in my life, I mean the business but not Sanju as he was not going to give up on our relationship nor miss any opportunities to make me feel guilty about what had happened to him and his hard work. Unbelievable you may think!

You may ask, what will it take to open my eyes?

There is more to follow on from this last saga with Sanju, the man of my dreams whom I am madly in love with. This tall, dark, handsome, liar, fraud, abusive, devil in disguise walking and talking the language of love and caring but all the while stabbing me in the back. This is so exciting; I need more of this intoxication to keep me hooked.

4: BEING STALKED

(Sanju the stalker, though I did not realise at the time)

After the embarrassing experience connected to the bankruptcy procedures, I did not want to have anything to do with Sanju and refused to answer his phone calls. Sanju being Sanju was not going to give up easily and started to hang around outside my home sitting in his van for hours hoping to get a glimpse of me, looking for a chance to worm his way back into my life. Worm his way he did. After all that happened, I was still in love with him, felt sorry for him and forgave him. Watching him sitting outside my house for hours melted my heart. I was also aware of the neighbours watching and wondering what they be thinking or talking about. At this stage of my life, it did not occur to me that I was being stalked; he turned up everywhere even when I took the dog for a walk, he was there in front or walking behind me. Shopping at our local supermarket was another target but he did this when I was on my own never when with my family or anyone else. He could have been there but did not come forward as he did when I was on my own. I should have set the dog on him, as if I would!

Eventually, I let him back into my life. It beggar's belief but I was still in love with him.

New chapter in our lives followed.

After the bankruptcy, both of us worked hard to re-build our careers and with encouragement from me Sanju went from strength to strength ending up working for one of the world class car-parts manufacturing company earning a handsome salary and undertaking an MBA at a prestigious University in the Midlands.

I too went on to work for a renowned IT & Management Consultancy Organisation. Both my sons excelled at their education and went on to prosper. Sanju later changed jobs and went to work in Dartford, Kent and before long we bought a beautiful, new build townhouse. It was seven years later before I moved in with him due to my work commitments in the Midlands.

5: FURTHER TALES OF WOES

(Move to Dartford)

I remember the day I left Birmingham, after seven years of having bought a home in Dartford; I was feeling sad because I had lived there ever since I arrived in the UK from East Africa. During my journey to Dartford, I was quite and when Sanju asked the reason I told him I was already missing my home and burst out crying. We stopped at a motorway service to talk with me fully expecting Sanju to understand my predicament but as we started talking about it, he became very emotional, and he *started to cry*. I thought he was crying because he felt sorry for me but was taken aback when he said that he was worried about the adjustments _he_ would have to make to accommodate me after all he had been living independently for seven years. This was not the start I had expected. 'A warning bell was already ringing in my head for me to take notice.'

Confused about who was supposed to comfort who and about what? During our conversations at the Motorway Services, I got the impression he was willing me to turn back. To go back to Birmingham. We continued with our three hours long journey to Dartford arriving late in the evening.

Our home was few miles outside Dartford and on a new housing estate. The surroundings were picturesque, remote, rural, and peaceful compared to Birmingham. It took some time getting used to my new surroundings and life. The bus service was on an hourly basis with some services not running regularly meaning if one bus was missed it meant a two hour wait. However, there was a man-maned train station about 15 minutes' walk from home, but I was not used to travelling by trains, mostly by car or occasionally by bus. I did not have a car, so had to travel by bus or get a lift from Sanju whose company, surprisingly, was only 10 minutes' drive from home.

First things first, I registered at the un-employment office and began my job search in earnest. On a weekly basis I was applying for twenty jobs in and around Dartford but without much luck, so I decided to venture further afield and before long secured a job with a company based in London. Though something out of my comfort zone, I accepted this job because I was beginning to struggle financially, and my savings were dwindling fast. Sanju was not forthcoming with any support and unlike before I moved in with him, he used to leave loose change lying around the house that I started using but making sure of letting him know. Soon that change became scarce as he decided to leave it in his office drawer instead. I think he enjoyed watching me struggle and ask, beg him for money. I felt alone and in despair, we were meant to be a couple but only when it suited him and especially not now when I was unemployed, and he was footing the bills.

One Saturday afternoon whilst out shopping for new clothes for him in the city centre, I excused myself making a dash to one of the counters in the Debenhams retail store, to withdraw some cash on my credit card and ran next door to a Bank to make an invoice payment. Felt a relief knowing there would be no overdue payment charges incurred. On returning to where Sanju was in the clothing store, he was busy looking at the shirts and trying to match ties. He had not noticed I was missing but as soon as he spotted me, he waved me over asking for help in deciding which shirt he should purchase. Imagine, how I was feeling seeing him at the same counter where I withdrew cash from Debenhams card to pay an invoice next door at the bank. Seeing him paying for his expensive shirts and ties, chosen by me, brought tears into my eyes. I was living in a parallel universe seeing him spending freely whilst I languished in near poverty. Sanju, after making the purchases turned round asking if I needed anything. The ask was there but not the intention because before I could reply he was marching towards the exit telling me he was famished. I dutifully followed him struggling to keep up. As he was paying the bill, he chose the eating venue. Whatever or wherever his choice of venue for lunch, it was beyond my capacity to pay or to offer a contribution. He introduced me to Nando's restaurant recently opened in Dartford City Centre.

Unfortunately, whilst Sanju lavished himself with expensive clothes and food, I was languishing in poverty dependent on benefit payments. Even weekly food shopping with Sanju, became a mundane outing as all I could do was watch him pick food stuff, place it into the trolley that I pushed round. I did not have the guts to select or have any cravings. No sooner did we get home; he would dump the shopping on the kitchen floor and disappear off upstairs leaving me to put it away and get on with the cooking. I was not in a good place, hundreds of miles from the Midlands, no family, friends, or money, totally dependent on Sanju who seemed to relish his newfound power, dominance over me. All I could do was bade my time and get a job, sooner the better. It was a not a pleasant setup, not a happy environment and I was beginning to dread our weekly shopping trips be it to the supermarkets or to purchase small or larger item for *our* home. Sanju, again, became abusive, shouting at me in the middle of the shop making me burst out crying and then molly coddling me saying he did not understand why I was making him angry with my behaviour. Truth be told, he did not have a clue about purchasing items such as furnishing or white goods or decorative items for *our* home so behaved in a manner to hide his lack of knowledge or experience. I knew it but because I loved him it was my duty, I felt, to not make him feel embarrassed or a novice, and in so doing kept taking the 'bullets' to protect his inflated ego. You see, he was not used to the prosperous lifestyle he was now living and was leaning heavily on me to keep him aware. I was excusing his narcistic behaviour and explaining it away. Somehow, I knew I was superior to him so did not need to show off or explain myself but then why was I getting upset with his brutal treatment of me. Why was I not able to manage it or put him in his place? I chose not to because I was not working and dependent on him. My main priority was to secure a job.

Hence, securing this job in London was not a choice but important to get back on my feet. I had a mortgage on property in Birmingham and other associated costs to meet plus being on benefits was destroying my self-esteem and confidence that was slowly being eroded. Sanju's negative behaviour was hard to ignore or walk away from. Foolishly, I convinced myself that his 'behaviour' may be due my dependency on him because he was well settled, earning good money, had a nice house, (his house nor ours).

The job offer in London was well-paid, higher status within a well-established public sector organisation, with additional benefits & rewards, and working from home optional. Whilst Sanju pretended to be pleased for me it was patently obvious he was struggling to accept the fact that I would be earning more than him and working from home. That did not go down well with him as he tried his best to avoid talking about my new job whereas had previously bored me to tears talking about his job and how well he was doing. End of the day, Sanju was a male chauvinist, and none of the women in his family held any jobs apart from sewing clothes for factories at home.

Strange how the very things that attracted Sanju to me, were also ones that threatened his inflated ego and possible loss of control over me.

I was flushed with happiness, singing and dancing around the house. So relieved, a bit apprehensive though but overall grateful for this wonderful break.

6: STARTING A NEW JOB

(At a public sector organisation)

Day came and I started my job and travels to and from London. At first it was unnerving, just thinking about the journey I felt butterflies in my stomach. Leaving home at around 6 am and getting back at 7:30 pm, the travel from Dartford to White City meant going to Charing Cross, then walking short distance to catch two further underground trains to my destination, White City. On my first morning of travel, I got off at London Bridge, came outside and was totally bewildered as to which way to turn. Luckily, the first person I stopped to ask for directions was heading to White City and asked me to follow him. I was a few minutes late getting to work.

My first day was as usual spent meeting my work colleagues and writing out my own induction plan as I became aware of the chaotic nature of the environment and its management. I was determined to hit the ground running, taking responsibility of meeting and greeting staff members. Meeting with my immediate manager proved useful and he gave me permission to leave early to get home at a reasonable time. Soon this meant arriving at 10 am and leaving at 4 pm and working from home, only coming into office when necessary. What a relief and a blessing this turned out to be. It did not take me long to settle into my new job and enjoy the freedom and responsibility that came with it.

Without realising it, I had fulfilled one of my wishes of working in London and travelling on the underground trains. I remember watching the news or films and seeing the hustle and bustle of men dressed in smart suits, wearing bowler hats, carrying a brief case and one of those long umbrellas. I used to be well impressed and wondered what it would be like to be part of that scenario. Something, at that time, far from my reach or reality. Yet here I was playing an active part in my own film; smartly dressed, carrying a laptop bag, documents holder and jumping on and off the London underground trains. I was in awe and wonderment seeing myself walking past Madam Tussauds or the Houses of Parliament on my way to attend a meeting. Having to attend the London Stock Exchange to ensure our organisation was efficiently managing the outsourced functions and overseeing our response to managing major incidents and outages.

As time went by, I became aware of a laid-back attitude of staff members to the point of missing their targets and job requirement. Unfortunately, my own manager was part of the problem, coming in late, smelling of drink, his unprofessional behaviour during meetings, spending more time on small talk, ignoring the items on the agenda. Therefore, it was no surprise that some of his staff members and my colleagues carried the same attitude encouraging him to focus on un-important discussions. Having previously worked for a world class private organisation and been trained on being client-driven and delivering quality. Moreover, in the private sector organisation, focus was on setting and meeting, even exceeding, customer expectations, avoiding penalties for non-compliance of contractual obligations.

Smart Aleck- Me not Them

During my induction process, my manager invited me to attend monthly Performance Review meeting with one of our key service provider intentions being that I would be conducting future meetings. Having arrived promptly, the meeting started late because no room had been booked for the meeting. When the meeting finally started, I was introduced as the newbie person who would be taking over the monthly performance meetings. At the close of the meeting as most attendees were desperate to get away to grab lunch at the local pub, I politely asked their head of IT to hold back for a few minutes. No sooner were we on our own, the first thing I said to him was, 'What was all that about?' The IT bod looked puzzled, but I repeated the question. He replied by asking me another question? Where I was from meaning which organisation I had worked for previously. When I told him, his response was 'Oh shit', immediately apologising for his off-handed behaviour and attitudes during the meeting further confessing that if the customer, meaning my manager and head of another department, haven't got a clue about their requirements than why would he, as the provider, bother either. I laid down the ground rules for any future meetings agreeing on my part, to provide clarity about our requirements and expectations. Notably, this type of behaviour was widespread with other providers with some having serious unresolved issues between providers resulting in a backlog of work that was not being reviewed or resolved.

Within a few months of my new role, providers roles and responsibilities were clarified and way forward agreed.

My 'hit the ground running' approach was beginning to achieve results positively impacting client, provider relationships. Whilst this was perceived as an excellent achievement for both the business and its services providers, some of my colleagues known for being unable to manage their part of the contract, including my own manager, were starting to behave negatively, ignoring me, not inviting me to their meetings, withholding vital information etc.

I soon learnt the meaning of 'no one likes a smart Alek'. Instead of being patted on the back for improving providers performance and delivery, I was beginning to rub people up the wrong way, both within my organisation and externally. Since, the failures in service delivery were everywhere, within the organisation and external providers, with me coming in demanding providers improve their process, procedures and systems, was groundbreaking changes. These changes flagged up internal staff weaknesses and insecurities especially as some had been with the organisation for many years, in some cases 5 to 9 years.

They were not up to the jobs, not skilled or reskilled, but because the fish was rotten at the top, most were riding high on the fact they were the 'owners, managers of the businesses and providers were answerable to them. Answerable to what or how when most were lacking in management skills, did understand the workings of the contract or what they were supposed to be performance reviewing. Complacency was deep rooted, incompetence levels visibly high, most were out of their depth dependent on the providers say-so.

I was willing to support them, being a new-recruit, I was seen as an outsider, my skill sets, experience, background were ignored only seen as someone responsible for upsetting their smooth operations. One of their so-called projects had been in the pipeline for four years and had an external consultant working on it making shed loads of money!! He too felt threatened with my level of expertise and experience. Shamefully, my days at this organisation were numbered because too many people felt exposed. Whilst I tried my best to be supportive, I was being pushed towards their ways of working and keeping the status-quo. This was a public-sector organisation, the ramifications for staff members not delivering or meeting their targets was washed over yet most were entitled to regular pay increases and bonus. Bonus for what?

I had worked hard to achieve my professional standards including a Master's in Business Administration (MBA) that took me 3.5 years to complete because I was working full time. In my previous organisation, after work, I stayed up late at night taking various IT courses to upskill and be better at my job, this helped to improve communication and connections with the IT staff, also known as techies. It was my responsibility to improve my skills, unlike staff at this organisation who saw it as their right to challenge but not be challenged, regardless.

7: TRAIN BUDDIES

The positive aspect of my daily train commuting was my bonding with three great, fun-loving commuters; Caroline who worked for a publishing company, Zofia was a recruitment consultant responsible for recruiting medical staff from Poland and Robin a friend of Caroline, but I never got to find out about his profession. We would mostly meet travelling back home in the evening's and soon became good friends looking forward to meeting and chatting all the way back. Whoever arrived first at the station, would save seats on the train for the others by placing items on them. Our regular meetings provided for a light-hearted break from our mundane often stressful jobs, as all we would do was crack jokes and laugh.

Sorry to admit sometimes, when one of our friends was missing and seat was taken up by another commuter, we tried to engage them in conversation including when a famous face sat on the empty seat, we tried to engage them in too. Hilariously, when a stranger asked if he could occupy the empty seat, we kindly gestured for him to sit. He complied, sat down, pulled out his lap-top busying himself. That day our conversation somehow tuned into talk about the 'Burkinis,' we seriously discussed its known uses, designs, marketing and which one of us could be a suitable model.

Without any hesitation Robin our guy was deemed most suitable, accompanied by chortling of laughter breaking out us at the thought of seeing him in a Burkini. I have no idea why we nominated him but that is how ridiculous our discussion was. Suddenly, we heard an unfamiliar laughter, curiously we looked at each other and then at the stranger who occupied the empty seat. He was in stiches, pretending to hide his face in his laptop than confessing he had never heard such a funny conversation, adding that he tried his best not to listen, but the on-going conversations were difficult to ignore. Such was the silly banter between us that even strangers got a laugh out of it.

At another time my commuting team felt I would make a good politician and tried their level best at convincing me to stand as a local MP, promising to cover the costs and marketing or promotion. My confession made them shake their heads in dismay, throwing their hands in the air and calling me a spoilt sport. I confessed to making a lousy MP because I was too honest, caring and would want to be effective. All three agreed with me. Compliment or an insult I am not sure, but we laughed it off as another half-baked silly idea.

As weeks rolled into months, I began to relax and enjoy my commute and the job, through stressful, provided a challenge and opportunity to use my skills and experience gained in previous roles elsewhere.

8: FALLOUTS - RELATIONSHIP UNTENABLE

Regrettably, the other reality of my life was quite different from my entertaining journey back home from work with my train buddies.

Sanju, who never made me feel well come since moving from Birmingham to Dartford, was becoming grumpier by the day about anything and everything. Even though I was the one leaving home early, travelling long distances, whilst his job was a mere ten minutes by car, but judging by his behaviour you would think he was the one leaving early and getting back late. As mentioned before, I was on a higher salary than him and working for a prestigious company with a few extra benefits thrown in including given an interest free loan to buy my train pass for the year deductible from my monthly salary.

He was beginning to show signs of jealousy making silly remarks about my salary being paid from his hard-earned money, he made snide remarks on a regular basis and was least interested in my actual day-to-day work but made a point of telling me how stressful and challenging his was. Admittedly, Sanju was struggling to accept that I was a higher earner than him. He was determined to put me my place in the house, his house as he referred to it since he had been living there longer. At the weekends, he expected me, like a good stay-at-home spouse, to clean the house, cook meals and do other chores whilst he disappeared for hours playing cricket and going for a pint with his mates afterwards.

When we came home after doing our weekly household shopping, he persistently dumped it in the hallway and go upstairs to put his feet up leaving me to put the shopping away and cook the meal. When I tried asking him for help, he would get moody, start shouting and accusing me of making his life difficult, as if he did not have enough on his plate. *Enough of what is what he did not clarify*. I soon realised his bad boy behaviour was a stich-up to wind me up; to cause a scene whereby he would do his usual shouting and swearing, calling me names and show no respect for himself or me. Bottom line is, he was looking for a way to create a negative environment, get me upset, then blame me for upsetting him and throw in the bit about me getting big headed because of my job.

I was not sure how to respond, you see he was an expert manipulator, and I did get caught out repeatedly because of my good nature also not one who liked conflict. There was a deep-seated childhood trauma or incident that made me averse to dealing with conflict, I would rather all was peaceful and be happy but at what cost to me and my good nature you may ask? Or was there another reason for his strange behaviour?

As mentioned earlier, I would leave home for work between 6 to 6:30 am and get back as late as 7:30 pm some days. Sanju's office was ten minutes away so he would leave at around 8:45, sometimes come home for lunch and be back by 5:15.

What did he get up to when he was home alone because he certainly did not have a meal waiting for me when I got back. Some days we would suffice by having a bowl of cereal for dinner.

As a matter of curiosity when I checked the history of sites visited on our home computer, I was horrified to discover he was habitually visiting pornographic material online. What Sanju had forgotten was that I knew a great deal about computers and looking at the computer's history was able to identify all the websites he had visited that were mostly pornographic by nature. Once when I was away for the weekend but came back earlier than expected he seemed very cagey. When I went upstairs to use the computer, I saw names, telephone numbers scribbled on a piece of paper of Asian Babes. Though tempted, I did not dare to call the numbers to verify for fear of finding out the truth. Not something I was not prepared to deal with. No sooner had I walked back into our home, I sensed someone had been there, it was my gut feeling and seeing the names and telephone numbers made me realise he had a visitor(s). Did not take much imagination to establish who or what went on whilst I was away.

Sanju had recently boasted about a fellow colleague whose daughter was interested in him and how on occasions had come to change clothes at our place for work related night outs. Your guess is as good as mine as to the true nature of her visits. As time went by atmosphere at home was becoming more hostile making me feel as if I was an outsider or a visitor. I was not allowed to change or re-arrange the fixtures or furniture without his permission and whenever we went shopping to buy household stuff, he had the final say to buy or not. I remember when we went to purchase household lamp shades, his boorish behaviour made me burst out crying in the lightning department of the store.

As was usual; after upsetting me, he was full of apology expecting everything to be all right demanding I cheer up. Even parking the car and coming out of the car park, he would get abusive if I turned right instead of left. All this was beginning to affect my mental health and wellbeing. I was working long hours, away from my loved ones, did not have any friends close-by to confide in.

One Saturday evening after returning home from shopping with him refusing to lift a finger expecting to be served, I became upset and decided to go for a walk rather than stay at home. I walked and I walked, crying all the while without realising where I was going. When I got tired of walking, I did not have a clue where I was and tried to identify any landmarks that I thought I recognised to make my way back. There were none! When I looked around, I could not see anything, it was pitch dark. A deep sense of trepidation overwhelmed me. Where am I? I slowly walked forward, half expecting to trip over and fall face down as ground under my feet was gravelly, uneven. I tried to stretch my hands forward to feel for things and then to my side, only to touch what seemed like a hedge.

That is good, I thought, keep feeling it and walking forwards, it is bound to come out somewhere and sure enough I could see a light burning ahead and walked towards it and as I approached it, I realised it was a barn. I sensed a familiarity about the area, looking to my right side, there was another barn with its doors open and I could see tractors inside. I was still feeling dis-oriented and walking past both the barns on either side of me. I continued walking straight ahead until I heard another familiar sound of a stream flowing. I quickly walked towards the sound, soon found myself standing on a bridge with stream running below it. There was a silver light streaking over the water, coming from the moon up above. Phew! I felt relieved because I knew where I was, and it happened to be the countryside stream I walked past most mornings heading to the train station.

Most mornings I would leave home 15 minutes earlier, rather than wake Sanju up to drop me off at the station. Walking out of my front door, I would turn right, come to the end of my road, then turn left walking past a beautiful park. So calm, quiet, serene, dewy grass, sun shining through the blades of the branches of the trees. It was paradise on earth, my paradise I got to experience leaving early. Coming to the bottom of this road, encountered a T-junction, crossing over, waking a few yards then approaching a sharp left turn into a narrow country road. Though walking down this road was dangerous due to its narrowness and sharp bends, I enjoyed fresh air with open countryside views all around. Sound of approaching cars meant immediately stepping aside to let them pass. Often, I would get a horn pipped at me, more to say thank you or acknowledge my presence. This was the same road that Zofia, a Polish Recruitment Consultant working in the city's husband used to drop her at the train station, honking to say hello and see if I wanted a lift. I would wave them on because I made two stops before getting to the station.

First stop was on this very bridge that I used to crossover to from houses with very narrow pavements. Only one person at a time could walk on these pavements. I would crossover and stop on the bridge to watch the stream flowing with fauna growing along its the sides. This was my second paradise after the park early in the morning, so beautiful, peaceful, and calm just what I appreciated before the hustle bustle of working in the city. I would stand here admiring the serenity of the view, breathing in fresh air before moving onwards to the newsagent's shop near the station. Approaching the shop, the smell of fresh baking wafted in the air. I was tempted to buy some pastries but resisted saying it was too early, and I already had some breakfast. I would walk in and have a quick five-minute chat with the owner, pay for my newspaper and make my way towards the station a few yards away.

The platform for the London bound train was on the opposite side, meaning walking over a bridge to reach it. I had seen some idiots rather than walk across the bridge, try to squeeze a gap of the manned barriers. Sure, enough my train would trundle into the station, never seemed to be in a rush, giving passengers, even late comers, ample time to clamber on board to be seated. The train made several stops before finally arriving at Charing Cross Station in London unloading its rush hour commuters hurriedly disappearing in various directions.

Returning to the here and now, after finding myself lost in the pitch darkness and using various senses to feel my way through full of trepidation, here I was standing at the same spot on the bridge. An eerie feeling enveloped me, due to the stillness, quietness of this place apart from sound of the stream running. I stood there somehow relieved, scared knowing the journey back was going to be problematic given it was dark, and I had left my phone at home. The heaviness of my feet placed firmly on the bridge gave me the grounding and inspiration to lift my feet one at a time and move forward. There was no other way accept retracing my footsteps back to the way I had just come though.

Though familiar with the narrow country road, it was a lonely, scary place to be walking in especially at night-time by myself. I looked around expecting Sanju to come looking for me but no luck. What do I do? I must get back but how? If only I had my phone, I could have used the torch light. Very reluctantly, I turned round and started walking towards the dark, narrow country lane thinking that if any cars came by, I would be able to catch their headlights. So, I felt safe in that sense. I was not aware of any dangerous animals in that area and the farm animals were safely locked away for the night.

As I approached the country lane, I was beginning to feel cold, shivery, scared and started running towards the T-junction at the end of the road. I could hear my heartbeat getting faster. I hoped and prayed there weren't any prowlers out. I ran as fast as my little legs could carry me, tripping over something in the road sending me flying. I face planted on the road, quickly got up without checking for any injuries, running faster than before wanting to make it before something goes wrong, though what, I was not thinking clearly only that I did not want anything to happen or go wrong now that I knew the T-junction was a short way away. The short distance seemed longer and never ending. Thank goodness, I did come to the end of the long winding and seemingly dangerous country road. I bent over with relief to try to catch my breath than crossing the road started making my way home walking past houses, staying clear of the park on the right side of the road. Feeling a sense of relief turning into my road and walking up my garden path.

Coming to the house, I rang the bell. Sanju came to the door and asked where I had been. I said that I had been for a walk and that seemed fine with him. I went upstairs to wash and get ready for bed. Slipping into bed, I was relieved to be home shaking my head at the horrendous experience I'd had, though feeling insecure about my relationship with Sanju various questions swirled round in my head but I felt exhausted after my nightmare experience of getting lost. I was too tired to care or think. No sooner had I put my head down on the pillows, I was knocked out. Waking up next morning, I was overcome by thoughts of my troubling relationship and where it was heading. I got up showered, got ready and went downstairs to get some breakfast as I was feeling famished. No sign of Sanju who was still asleep, though in separate bed upstairs.

As usual, my relationship with Sanju was not getting any easier it seems he was looking for any and every excuse to get upset or have an argument, even simple things like me reading 'his' newspaper before him was tantamount to major upset. When he had his meal, he would walk off the table without helping me clear up or wash up and if he decided to eat in the lounge upstairs, he would leave the tray on the floor. A few times I did ask him to take it downstairs, but he ignored me and when I refused to clear up after him, his dishes were left in the lounge for days with him stepping over them to reach for something on the lounge table. Whether deliberate or habitual, his behaviour was destabilizing me. I could not relax, enjoy watching television or making any phone calls with him around. When someone called him, he would leave the room and return when his call ended.

I worked hard to clean and tidy up our home and once when the garden had been properly tended, I heard myself saying that everything was picture perfect by that I meant inside the house had been newly refurbished and plants and flowers planted in the garden and beautiful hanging baskets hung by the front door. Other than that, my life was empty, I was struggling to settle down as Sanju's behaviour made it nearly impossible for me to feel at home. On a monthly basis after work, I would catch a train to Birmingham and return to Dartford after work on Monday evening.

Life at home, in Dartford, was not getting any easier. Sanju stayed up late every night on pre-text of watching television and only came upstairs when I fell asleep. Eventually, getting fed up with his deliberate actions of avoiding coming to bed until I fell asleep, I made an excuse that I did not want to disturb him in the mornings and started sleeping in the spare bedroom on the second floor. Some nights, due to the disturbing situation at home, I lay awake planning my escape and thoughts of packing my bags, calling a taxi and leaving without saying goodbye. I was thoroughly miserable, from being a positive, happy go-lucky person, the negative environment in my home was making me unwell.

Whenever I tried to talk about the beautiful weather to make conversation, he sarcastically responded I visit spec-savers. My dreams and expectations on moving to Dartford involved being out and about in the evenings, travelling to places like Ashford, Dover and Whitstable and going on the Eurostar to Paris, no chance. Even asking to take a walk around Dartford on Sunday's produced a negative response.

As for going out, once when we were invited to his manager's place for dinner, we promptly turned up at 7 pm and had a good evening but around midnight I started to get tired and a bit bored and besides I saw our host looking at his watch, so I nudged Sanju to leave. Leave we did but I got the silent treatment all the way home and no sooner had we entered our home, he started shouting and telling me off for embarrassing him in front of his manager. Why? By asking to leave when he was not ready or been asked to by his manager. Unbelievable, I thought, who does he think he is? To preserve my sanity, I went upstairs to bed. Not surprisingly, the next day Sanju gave me the silent treatment and only spoke when I asked him something. It was not looking good the situation was worsening with no respite in between. I was struggling to think what or why he is acting this way.

Then there was the phone call from his mother congratulating him on the birth of his nephew. He was abrupt and rude to his mother and could not wait to get off the phone. I too congratulated him on the birth of his nephew, but he stormed out of the room. How odd I thought?

Later, in my saga with Sanju, you will learn the truth about his reaction.

Soon after joining the Broadcasting Services, I got a pay rise and when I told Sanju he was not pleased and lectured me about public funds being misused. No thumbs-up, had that been him I would be expected to do the Congo dance around him. Being honest, I was beginning to get fed-up of trying to appease him whilst suspecting some sort of foul play was going on but unable to figure it out. Then one weekend when I came to Birmingham, he called to say his family was travelling the other way, from Birmingham to Dartford. I was not bothered because Sanju had not made any attempts to introduce me to his family or talk about them always re-iterating they would never accept me being a single parent was considered a disgrace, but ok for them to visit *my* home when I was not around.

When I returned home on Monday evening, *our* home felt different, and I soon found out why? Sanju, had moved all my belongings, hiding them from his family including my shoes, slippers, make-up. After their visit, his attempts at putting them back had failed miserably. I was livid, felt humiliated in my own home demanding to know what explanations he was going to provide. Instead of explaining his actions, Sanju launched into a furious tirade against me, blaming me for causing a rift with his family who thought I was not good enough for him forgetting the fact that he had middle class lifestyle, was living in Dartford thanks to my hard work and support. Oh no, Sanju was going the extra mile to ward me off saying that I was the worst thing that happened to him calling me ugly and old. I burst out laughing because I knew for fact that I was good looking and smart as compared to his simple folks, no airs or grace. He stepped forward and slapped me hard on my face forcing me to fall backwards on the floor, lashing out further by kicking and hitting me all the while shouting and no sooner had he stopped he made it out as if it was all my fault by saying, 'see, see what you made me do', 'why do you wind me up so much?' Calling me a wind-up merchant and left the room. I slowly got off the floor feeling badly shaken and bruised. I could feel blood dripping side of my lip. I wiped it and sat on the bed shaking. I wanted to run out of the house to my neighbours asking them for help and as I stood up, Sanju walked into the room full of apologies. He burst out crying saying that he could not believe what he had done to me and that it was unlike him. He came over hugging and kissing me promising to make things better for me saying he needed my help to control his temper. I wished he would leave me alone but as always; he was not going to until he got the reassurances that all was going to be fine, no problem, so what, only a few slaps and kicks, no harm done!!

This time, I pretended to go along with him even going downstairs to have dinner though struggling to swallow because my face was hurting, and I had a cut on my lip that was beginning to swell. Though, hurting all over especially my stomach, I did not show making an excuse to go upstairs. Changing into my nightie and pretending all was well between Sanju and me. He kissed me good night and asked if he could make me a mug of Horlicks to which I replied no thanks, turned to face the other way pretending to be sleepy. I heard the bedroom door open, turned round to see him leaving the room. I cried myself to sleep that night, waking up during the night due to aches and pain from the beating. Sitting up in bed forcing myself to face the truth of what had just happened and how I kept putting myself in danger of serious harm. What happened should not have come as a surprise after as I had received warnings of clear and present danger that I chose to ignore hoping, praying things would change or were not as bad as I had imagined them to be. Finally, shamefully, after receiving a brutal beating, I admitted to myself that I had been a fool for ignoring warning signs thinking that Sanju would/could one day change and worst still that I could change him. Throughout our relationship, I was the one who kept changing, adjusting, pretending, ignoring the truth and letting him walk all over me.

Why? The same adage.

Because I loved him, foolishly believing he was my soulmate, his saying, my one and only true love. By believing thus, I let him use me and abuse me. Another realisation was that Sanju tried his level best to demean me and destroy my self-esteem, to bring me down on my knees.

That night I relived the horrors of some of the terrible situations I had been through and how repeatedly made excuses for his bad behaviour. It dawned on me that it was Sanju who had stolen the money from my handbag and was prepared to see me spend time in a prison cell. Thanks to him, I lost my home because he pressured me to get Kamal to sign over the home to me, but Kamal was clever, he instead defaulted on the mortgage payments leading to our family home being re-possessed. Then there was the bankruptcy brought on due to thousands owed to banks and other creditors. I blamed myself for trusting Sanju but at the same time I was working seven days a week, had a young family and because we were not living together there had to be an element of trust between us. Sanju was very convincing, promising to be everything Kamal was not and look after me and the children. Sanju, was a narcissist, far worse than worse than Kamal who never lifted a finger on me or the children. Sanju was protective of his own family, constantly making excuses for keeping our relationship secret and carrying on same pattern when I moved in after seven years of living apart. He would never sacrifice his family the way I had done including, though sounding foolish now, standing up to my extended family and revealing my love for Sanju. Literally beating the drum about my love for him.

I left Birmingham to come to Dartford, focused on getting a job in London doing a daily commute, never complaining about being tired or struggling to cope.

Whereas Sanju's office base was a ten minutes' drive, no threats of any hold-up or being late for work. He casually would leave home at around 09:45 to start work at 09:00 hrs and be back home by 5:30 pm. Most evening when I got back home, he expected a cooked meal and to up after him. On days, he had to provide a meal we would either end up having bowl of breakfast cereal or beans and chips.

What a heavy price paid for love and thinking he loved me too. The shame brought on by realisations that I repeatedly fell for his sweet talk, ignoring, as I did before, the warning signs. Trusting him when he had bankrupted me and allowed him to abuse and terrorise me into submissions. On several occasions when he was being negative or moody, I remember walking behind him and looking at the back of his head thinking to myself that he was the devils incarnate. The Satan!

That night after the beating, I finally admitted that he was not a good person to be around, and I needed to get away. I cried so much that night but making the decision to leave him brough a sense of calmness and hope into a hopeless situation. The question was how and when, but it had to be sooner than later? In fact, I felt spending another day with him could be fatal if he sees through my pretence.

9: WAKING UPTO REALITY

As morning came, I got up and got ready for work packing some extra clothes into my rucksack and laptop bag. Looking at myself in the mirror it was not a pretty site, I had to get away, leave now before it was too late. As I came downstairs to have a cup of tea and some cereal, Sanju was already awake apologising for his behaviour last night, making a fuss by offering to make me tea and toast. He looked at me and said that I should not go in today because I did not look well. I told him I had an important meeting to attend but he insisted I work from home and did a conference call instead. I explained my attendance was important at the meeting with key providers. Cheek of him telling me what I should do.

He insisted on dropping me off at the station and even carried my bags to the car. I was conscious of the fact that he was watching me all the time making me nervous. It was as if he was trying to read my mind. I was glad when we approached the station and I asked to be dropped off at the newsagents, he instead fetched the newspaper returning with some chewing gums and sweets for my journey. Walking me to the station and kissing me goodbye. I was glad to get away because I was not sure how much longer I was going to hold up the pretence. When he kissed me goodbye, handing my bags over to me, I walked away and did not look back aware that I was aching all over and just wanted to get away before Sanju realises something was wrong and stopped me from boarding my train.

I walked as fast as my little legs could carry me, up the stairs, walking cross the bridge over to the other side. I was desperate to put my bags down and find some place to sit but before I could do that, I heard the train approaching. Summoning all my strength, I grabbed my bags and walked towards the train, boarded it, found somewhere to sit, put my rucksack on the overhead space and slumped into my seat. Wishing, hoping not to bump into anyone as I was feeling awful and do doubt looked it but did acknowledge the person sitting opposite. I was on tenterhooks until the train pulled out of the station but relaxed only a bit because I knew the next stop was Dartford city another place someone who knew me could board. Pretending to be busy, I took my laptop out, logged on and placed a 'working from home' message on my work calendar, busied myself reading work emails in outlook and previously saved documents on my desktop. I gave up trying to work, put my laptop away and sat back, relaxing into the seat staring out of the window feeling miserable as hell. I was adamant not to give in to my fears or nasty thoughts about last night.

I closed my eyes and tried to have a rest, that proved easier than I thought as I soon dosed off waking up when I heard the ticket inspector calling out for tickets. I quickly sat up, rummaging through my handbag, producing my travel pass for checking. When I looked outside, the train was approaching Charing Cross. I disembarked and headed towards the overground train to Euston Station from where I got train to Birmingham New Street. I was heading back home to Birmingham and not going into work as I had assured Sanju. Arriving at Birmingham New Street, I made my way to the station café to take timeout before going home. I felt a sense of relief that I was home and safe from Sanju when the phone rang, and it was him. I was filled with intrepidation thinking he had followed me and could be watching me. I glanced over my shoulder to check ignoring his call.

Turning round, I felt huge amount of anger building up within me, it felt as if something was morphing uncontrollably within me. Its intensity was such that I wanted to let go, wanting to scream to release the pressure, the pent-up stress. I banged hard on the table with my right fist yelling out, 'how could you let the bastard treat you so badly?' I threw both my hands in the air, shaking my head and was about to let out another scream when I felt a hand on my shoulder. I froze thinking it was Sanju, slowly turning round was relieved to see it was a staff member come over to ask if I was ok. I nodded my head at the same time noticing I was wearing my earplugs and pulling them out apologised stating that one of my favourite songs was playing. In that moment I wished the earth would open so I could disappear. No such luck! The caring staff member gave me a stern look and walked away back behind the counter.

Looking round the café, it was full of customers of varying ages, and I noticed all eyes were on me, some showing concern whilst others shaking their heads in disgust. Sheepishly smiling, wording sorry with my lips, waving to them picking up my coffee slowly started sipping. It was piping hurt burning my lips. One quick glace over the counter and I was met with the same stern look from the Barista. Managing to compose myself, feeling calmer keeping my head down pretending to enjoy my drink feeling stupid. Slowly sipping my coffee thinking I should have gone to the police station to report the abuse realising also that would have kept me trapped in Dartford and be at the mercy of Sanju. Good move coming back to Brum, believing I was out of harms was, safe heading back to my one and only true home with my family.

I decided not to tell my son about the abuse only saying things did not work out and we decided to split up. Giving him an account of the abuse and how much and for how long I had been suffering was something I would struggle to explain. After all, I was his mother, someone he had profound respect and admiration for, his words. He could never imagine in a hundred years anything so horrific happening to me, their mother who had tried to shelter them from harm and harmful endeavours. I could not do this to him, so best to keep it secret. Getting up, picking up my bags I made my way to the Ladies to freshen up and apply some make up and lipstick. Leaving the station, made my way to the taxi stand, I was on my way home feeling nervous and anxious, aching all over with tears in my eyes struggling to come to terms with my terrible experience. I did my best to try to be cheerful not knowing if anyone would be at home.

Arriving home, I paid the taxi driver and walked slowly up the drive rumbling in my handbag for my house spare keys pulling out keys for the front door in Dartford. Sadness overcame me but I managed to find the house keys let myself. As luck would have it and to my relief, there was no one at home giving me enough time to settle down before my eldest son returns which he soon did. Walking in he was surprised to see me but equally happy. I briefly told him that I was going to be travelling to London from Birmingham to work because I had split up with Sanju. My son walked over and gave me a big hug assuring me we would talk later as been on a long journey and looking was tired. I duly went upstairs to my old bedroom putting my bags down, I looked round thinking, feeling it was indeed good to be home, this is where I belonged. Since moving to Dartford, it never felt like my home and Sanju made sure of that. Slumping on my bed, I fell into a deep sleep waking up early evening, feeling peckish. Going downstairs, my son welcomed me with a warm smile and a hug saying it was good seeing me. It was refreshing to be greeted with a smile and a hearty meal prepared by him. After the meal, I went into the lounge sitting down followed by my son who was keen to know if I was ok. We talked for a good hour only telling him that I had made a mistake moving to Dartford and Sanju was too set in his ways to consider that I may be struggling to settle down. I put my head back on the settee about to fall asleep when I realised, I needed to log on to check my work e-mails. There was plenty for me to tend to and phone calls to make. Work kept me busy for rest of the day catching up with the back log then logging out for the day. One of the benefits of working from home.

Later that evening my phone rang, and it was Sanju. I thought best to answer otherwise he would keep calling. He was outside the train station waiting to pick me up and wanted to know if I had missed the train and what time the next train gets in. Reluctantly, I told him I was back in Birmingham and will not be coming back. Preparing myself for an argument over the phone, he took me by surprise by saying it was my decision and one he deserved and with that he put the phone down. I felt confused and annoyed at not being given the chance of lay it into him after all during the day my mind had been practicing what to say and running all sorts of scenarios. Cannot be right Sanju putting the phone down on me. How was I going to come to terms with this? I was getting worked up thinking, expecting him to call back debating my response to his onslaughts over the phone, giving me the third degree, argue, shout, call me names.

He put the phone down, seems he was not surprised that cannot be right. My mind went into overdrive, talking to me, coming up with thoughts akin to mental and emotional torment. 'See even when he is not around, he has a hold on you', then in his defence thinking, 'How can it be his fault when he obviously sounded hurt over the phone?', and that I had acted in haste and should have gone back home (Dartford), to talk to him and given him a chance to explain himself and make amends. Slowly and surely my mind was making me out to be the villain and him the victim, the one who acted recklessly without thinking through the consequences of leaving poor Sanju all by himself. If I genuinely loved him than nothing was beyond forgiveness.

In my lifetime through my parents, religious teaching, and self-help books, I had come to believe that love and loving to be unconditional and if one person was wrong the other should rise above and be forgiving. Not to look for what was wrong with the other person but show understanding of their shortcomings.

10: WORKPLACE SHANANIGANS

(You come to work, think again. In some organisations job titles, egos, cliches and being team player are key, in other words not upsetting the apple cart)

Returning to my story about life without Sanju, coming back to Birmingham and leaving Dartford for good was painful. Remember, I walked away with clothes on my back and a few stuffed into my rucksack and laptop bag. First, on the weekend back at home, I went shopping for smart wear for work and invested in a pair of comfortable shoes and other essentials.

Coming back home meant I had to talk to my extended family and relations to put them into the picture. I got mixed reactions with most feeling sorry for me given the sacrifices I had made to make the move. A few weeks after my move back, one Saturday evening when I had visitors at home, the bell rang, my son answered the door, came back into the lounge, and said it was Sanju. I shook my head as I did not want to see him. Sanju had brought back my belongings and when my son told him I was not available, he deposited my belongings on the doorstep and promptly left. I felt a pang of guilt for being rude but reminded myself he was not worthy of any more of my time or consideration.

Sanju did not give up and called me whenever he was in Birmingham begging to see me if only to go out for a meal for old times' sake.

As for commuting daily to London from Birmingham, was beginning to take its toll especially when daily there were problems with the trains due to usual excuses - problems with overhead lines, signals problems at Rugby, missing trains or leaves on the track. I was late getting to work, leaving early to try to get back home at a reasonable time but it was like trying to catch my own tail. Since breaking up with Sanju and doing the daily commute from Birmingham to London, began to show as I struggled to motivate myself or find the strength to continue.

As already mentioned, working for a public sector organisation was an opener. I was surprised at the way services were delivered and high level of dependency on the providers to deliver them effectively and with efficiency. That was not the case and holding a title of Head of Service Delivery, placed the responsibility squarely on my shoulders. In my previous jobs, as someone who held a brilliant record having worked as a service provider and customer, meaning having experience of being on both sides of the fence. In this role, here I was the customer. Easy job, one would think but on the contrary due to lack of controls and checklists being put in place, this place was a mess due to lack of staff experience and competence. Looking round the office, it looks busy or buzzing with activity, no sooner had I got my feet under the desk, initiated my own induction as none put in place, I was treading on eggshells, smiling a lot and biting my tongue.

Most staff members, same as the one of the provider's Head of It, treated me like a trainee, cancelling meetings at short notice without any explanations or submitting the required information or documents. Given the intensity of my role, I did not sit around but started floor walking to introduce myself, explain my role and expectations. Soon, I had gathered enough business intelligence to know what was going on or in some case not. Every day became a struggle be it the service provider or our own internal staff. The service providers had been given a free run to do pretty much as they wished. As per the contract, that I studied to understand my role, monthly reports and data was not forth coming and meetings were seen as place to have a laugh and joke. After a couple of meetings, I put a structure in place as to the content and context of these get togethers, stipulating monthly management reports to be submitted prior to the meeting and attendees be treated with respect and given a chance to have their say as a few were dominating meetings.

Guess what? Some of them gave a toss and it was business as usual for them. No prior reports, walking in unprepared, spending time talking gibberish, throwing paper planes at each other and poking fun at someone's new hairstyle or outfit. These were adults behaving like children. I was flabbergasted, took note and prior to next meeting sent out the same instructions as before adding a list of required attendees eliminating ones least contributing or needed. I did see changes taking shape apart from one of the key service providers choosing to ignore my instructions. On the eve of the next meeting when no reports were submitted, I sent out a notice cancelling it. I knew that would put the service provider in breach of their contractual agreements. This created a massive furore next day with my manager's phone ringing nonstop who came over to have a 'chat' with me telling me the service provider organisation has been badly impacted and that I should not have taken that step. This was the same guy who had been conducting these meetings for years: never read any of the reports, bothered if they were submitted, or noticed any issues. He did not have a clue what to look for or expect and the service providers knew it. His prime purpose was to look forward to the paid for drinks and meal and go back home. Total dereliction of duty. Here he was, unfortunately, as my manager come to tell me off, sort of. For what? Trying to do a job that I had been appointed to due to my work experience and skill sets. It was clear that he had not been reading his emails because I had copied him into emails sent to the service providers. Pointing to copy of the contract that clearly stated roles and responsibilities of internal staff members as well as provider organisations, I paused looking at him thinking, as the head of the department, he had come over to complain to me about my actions. Warning bells inside my head warned me to be careful. Unfortunately, rightly, or wrongly, I did not have much room for manoeuvre, so apologised to him, reminding him that he had been copied into emails and the service provider was in breach of his terms and conditions. To my surprise, he agreed with me saying they needed to pull their act together and left. Somehow, I did not believe him. If that was not enough, the head of the organisation's Risk Management rang to make an appointment with me explaining he needed an urgent meeting with me. I asked who else needed to be present and he replied to no one else. I duly informed my manager who expressed an interest in being present. I forwarded his details asking he speak to him directly. My manager was declined his request to attend. When the meeting took place, it was to inform me of serious concerns with regards to behaviour of individuals within my department that had set alarm bells ringing. When I pressed for further information, the staff member produced a list with names and of concerns. My manager's name was on top of the list, indicating his excessive drinking habit and being in attendance drunk or smelling of drink. I was asked if I had been aware, but I declined to comment instead asking what was expected of me. I was told that prior to an external Quality Audit an internal Audit was imminent, and a list of staff members was required to book them in for Risk Management training. I tried to hide glee at what had just transpired but kept a straight face. These requirements would add to my workload and place me in a confrontational situation as I had been sworn to secrecy due to its sensitivity and certain individuals being monitored, including my manager. Over the next few weeks, I met the challenges of requirements but not without meeting resistance and further complaints to my manager. When one of my staff members refused to comply, I sent an email to Head of Risk Management updating them and asking them to intervene directly which they did.

The Head of Risk Management, complemented at the speed and timely completion of their requirements including preparing and undertaking an internal Audit. Alas! this came at a big cost to my own position within the organisations. Close cliques developed, my team members hardly spoke to me, and information was withheld from me. I had become a pariah, and the extra pressures placed on me by the Head of Risk Management did not help. I was working with one hand tied behind my back, unable to explain or warn my team members due to being sworn into secrecy. Attending weekly team meeting was proving hard, felt like no one was interested in hearing what I had to say or share information. The worst culprit was my manager, who made it his duty to single me out for criticism whilst praising others where none was necessary. Attending meetings and being on-site were a façade with most ignoring me, talking and laughing out loudly to make it look as if they were having fun, unfortunately at my expense. I was beginning to feel the pressure, seeking outside staff members to have a conversation with or keeping my head down working at resolving service provider related problems. Fortunately for me, apart from the key service provider, others were compliant and started delivering positive results.

Once when the Head of Risk Management came to see me, I shared my concerns with him explaining that my situation had become untenable forcing me to consider resigning. I felt doing the job was not the problem, my own team had alienated me, and I was being ignored on a mass scale. Not only my job was suffering but it was having an impact on my health and wellbeing making me miserable at the thought of coming into work. He listened intently, then shaking his head he remarked that it was them who should be leaving. Most were utterly useless at their jobs, earning shed loads of money, spoilt rotten and caused untold security problems for the organisation. He singled out my manager for allowing his staff members a free hand and totally lacking in understanding of threats to the organisation that could result in hefty fines and penalties. He told me it had been a pleasure working with me and that I had been extremely helpful and professional. He soon left advising me not to resign but find another job elsewhere within the organisation. That day I left work feeling deflated thinking what good was being commended by others when my own colleagues chose to distance themselves from me.

I felt a sense of pride at having done a good job and held these individuals to account, including my manager. Through dedication, hard work, hitting the ground running and always willing to learn and ask awkward questions, had earned me the knowledge and experience used in my current role. Leaving would not be my loss but the organisation's. These individuals were hired to do a job but not being held accountable was foreign to me. Having worked for private organisations the focus was on efficient service delivery and bottom line i.e., profit generating. Here no one cared as it was the taxpayers and subscribers' money that was used.

When I handed my resignation, giving one month's notice, there was no resistance or discussion. My manager pretended to be surprised but he wasn't. From that point onwards, I worked rigorously to put structures in place, reviewed process and procedures, documents, updated schematics and constructed a filing system on the shared drive. I wanted to leave making sure documents and files had been updated and placed in the correctly named folders. I created a comprehensive list of contacts saving them to the shared drive.

Since handing my notice, my team members behaviour changed towards me. They became noticeable more friendly and chatty with me. This change was an essential part on their behalf as most had become aware of how much I had been doing, including their jobs, and wanted me to share that knowledge and information with them. I did not feel any animosity or remorse but felt sorry for them because I had set the precedence both internally and with external providers, they would have to comply with given that Risk Management was on the scene and expected monthly reports about risks and issues for their areas.

One of my key concerns was leaving a well-paid job and being unemployed. Thinking about all that I had put myself through trying to settle in Dartford and accepting this job required daily commute in and out of London. Being forced out of my home in Dartford due to abuse and indifference from Sanju and then travelling daily from Birmingham was tough. Whilst I enjoyed the job, I had not bargained for the team or group dynamics that put up so many barriers in my path. As the saying goes, 'birds of a feather flock together.' Their comfort zones had been threatened by me, and they were not having it. Overall, there was a clear message for me that finally made me hand in my notice. My health and wellbeing were more important than being on a treadmill just to please others. Enough was enough!

On my last day at work, the whole team turned up at the local pub for drinks and lunch! There had been a collection, and I was given a store voucher. After much merriment and speeches, unbelievable, we went back to the office. I handed over the organisation's laptop, bag, phone and badges. Making my way to the exit, I was met by the Head of Risk Management who came to say goodbye and handed over a gift wrapped present. He leaned forward, giving me a hug, wishing me all the best and saying I will be missed. That was touching! I looked back and saw my team standing by their desks waving to me, I waved back to them, called the lift, got in, pressed for ground floor and left the building feeling sad at the prospect of, in a way, having failed to deliver the required changes.

Once outside, I turned round wishing all who had crossed my path, well.

When my train arrived at Euston Station, Sanju was waiting at the platform and walked over, leaning over to give me a kiss but I pulled away. He did not look well and asked to have coffee with him, but I declined. He handed me a new mobile phone he had purchased to replace my work phone. I must admit, I was pleased at his kind gesture and thanked him. He again asked me to stop for a coffee, I again declined and said goodbye. Both went our own ways, him back to Dartford and me to Birmingham. Whilst on the train, I realised the reason he bought me the mobile phone? It was to stay connected and had already set it up. It was several months later whilst looking at the features of this phone, I was shocked to see Sanju had was tracking my calls meaning had activated calls pick-up or notification when someone called me. This meant he was able to pick up calls before and to my horror I noticed calls were being answered when I had not done so myself. Cynically, if calls had already been answered than I would not be picking them or know who had called. Within Settings on my phone, I located the feature he had turned on and switched it off. Knowing what had just happened sent a cold chill down my spine. It made me think he could be stalking me. I went to the window, looking outside was relieved to see no cars parked outside.

Another Job -now at the NHS

After a short break, I managed to secure a job with the NHS, though not high profile, it paid well and besides, I was through taking on any more stressful jobs or taking on too much responsibility. This job suited me to a tee. I could work from home or leave home early and get back before traffic jams occurred. I was working 7.5 hours, taking an hour's lunch break, and not committing to any overtime. Furthermore, any hiccups anywhere within the pipeline of the work schedule would be returned to the source or not get done. Seems, I had learnt the hard way, how not to work hard and try to be resolute like before. To be honest, staff at this organisation were no better than ones I left behind in London, key difference being this one was meant to be a caring place to work for, after The NHS was responsible for delivering public healthcare and treatment. No chance!

This new place of work was full of self-important individuals who did not walk but floated in the air due to their inflated egos. The way staff were treated depended on their grades and where this fitted in the hierarchy structure. Here to I hit the ground running difference being, it was not about the job but survival skills to keep ahead of the charades all round me. It was, 'Yes sir, no sir, three bags full sir' and what is it you want me to do and how much? Those reading may be appalled that I chose to conform, sell my soul, and not stand up to crass behaviours and lack of attention to details and deliverables. Like I said, it was a circus with busy bodies running hither and dither looking important, attending loads of meeting and the classic one was calling a meeting to discuss if a meeting needs to be scheduled. I sat there with a grin on my face and mumbling, stupid fools, under my breath.

The problem with this role was at my grade, I was considered subservient and not consulted for decisions making or required to make any. Another hilarious example to share was after a meeting, I was asked to create a Visio diagram of a workflow for a new process. In one of my previous private organisations, I was considered a whizz kid when it came to creating flowcharts, schematics and responsible for training others on creating them. Before the next meeting, I submitted the drawing to the secretary for distribution with other meeting documents. For this meeting, we were required to travel to Worcester. A good day was ahead with all expenses paid and lunch provided. Cut a long story short, one of the senior manager's, did not know how to use Visio and instead of asking me; to explain the diagram, he opened an XL Spreadsheet and spent the whole meeting re-doing it. I did feel upset but quickly reminded myself it was not worth me getting distracted. I sat there watching the whole meeting centred around this person's egotistical behaviour and dominance. Total waste of the organisation's time, money, and valuable resources, looking round the table with ten attendees, none had the gall to interrupt him or make any suggestions. Being the most senior manager, he treated the meeting as his fiefdom, no questions asked or interruptions. Outcome of the meeting was that he re-assigned the drawing to two contracted management consultants in attendance. These guys belonged to a well-known management consultancy that I was aware of, and their modus operandi was to send any drawings, documents to a call centre in India where they would be worked on and sent back within a day using the time difference between India and UK. How so? No sooner the meeting ended, the information was emailed to Indian colleagues who worked on it whilst we slept and dropped into their inboxes before work started following day.

At this stage in my life, safe to say, I was content with my job that worked around my needs and paid me well. Though no match for experience and status, I had come to terms and wanted a peaceful, stress-free life. Sorry to admit but I had leaned the tricks of the trade and looked after myself only doing what I was asked to do and let the big chiefs rule their fiefdoms smoking the peace pipe with them whatever the cost to the organisation.

11: SANJU TRUTH REVEALED

The same applied to my relationship with Sanju, not bothered, looking after number one that is me.

I met him on my terms when he visited his family in Birmingham whilst still living and working in Dartford. Out of sheer curiosity, to tag him along and in a way get my revenge on him, I decided to meet him once a month when he drove down to see his family. Our relationship was cordial, no string attached. We would meet up, go for a meal or to the movies but I could not help noticing a subtle change in Sanju's mannerism. He seemed to be in a rush to get back home making excuses like he forgot his keys at home, needed to get back early or one of his parent's was unwell or his brother was coming back early from his taxi driver's job to spend time with him and so on. He also talked a great deal about his niece and nephew. He thought the world about them and worried about their future given the restricted environment both were growing up in. I listened but did not make any comments as I was not interested, keener on knowing what his game plan was so, I had a gut feeling he was up to something but did not let on or discuss.

One day when he was in Birmingham, we met up to go to the movies, but he seemed a bit distant, pre-occupied. After the watching a movie, Sanju was in a rush to get back to his parents and was not at all interested in spending any further time with me. He drove straight back to my place to drop me off without saying a word, parking outside my home. I got the impression he wanted me to leave so he could drive off. Bemused, by his strange behaviour, I picked my handbag, opened the car door and as I was about to step outside, Sanju suddenly spoke saying he was sorry for being quiet. He continued stating with a serious voice the reason was due to worry about his newborn nephew's on-going health problems including refusing milk. I must admit I was not overly bothered given his brother and sister-in-law were the parents looking after him, not him. I was getting a bit irritated thinking it was another excuse; his face was sombre. I sat back in my seat putting my hand on his arm saying that I was sorry to hear about his nephew and that he was safe adding his brother and sister-in-law are with him. He snapped at me saying angrily that as usual I was not concerned and demanding to know what made me think he was fine. I looked at Sanju trying hard not to smile as I found the whole tale funny, but he looked away shaking his head in disgust at my non-caring attitude. I said goodbye, stepped out of the car feeling confused about what just happened, shaking my head I walked away without looking back. Walking towards my front door, I analysed what had been said. Sanju shared his main concern about his nephew's ill health and refusing milk. A widespread problem with young babies and one that can be resolved with help from their family doctor or local Heath Visitor. Once indoors, I sat down feeling a bit confused, shaking my head in disbelief at Sanju's latest performance?

Why was Sanju so bothered about his nephew talking as if he were his dad?

As if by magic a thought came to my mind. I thought about my thinking that it was absurd cannot be true, or was it? Was I being stupid, ridiculous, even allowing myself to think it. I knew it was true. OMG! My light switch moment!

He is not; I called out; tell me it is not true that he is the father of this child. I knew then it was the truth but was not going to waste any more of my time thinking about it apart from laughing aloud at the realisation. I remember saying aloud 'sod' you and your problems Sanju. Then going upstairs, I got ready for bed, climbed into my bed, and had a good night's sleep.

However, on waking next morning, the events of previous night were in the forefront of my mind as I lay in bed thinking. Does this mean his nephew and niece were his children. He has been sleeping around with his own sister-in-law! His sister-in-law, his brother's wife, how can that be possible? Never heard of anything like it before in my life and yet his reality was staring me in the face. How? When? Did his family know? This was too interesting to let go off, I needed to spend time finding the underlying cause of the revelation, no proof, my gut feeling was telling me that it true.

My reasoning went as follows as pieces of the jigsaw started to fit together. Sitting back comfortably on my lounge settee with a cuppa tea and some biscuits, the thoughts and parallel came flooding in.

I recalled Sanju, a while ago telling me about his family problems particularly to do with his younger sister-in-law being unable to conceive and undergoing IVF treatment. I remember him telling me that his mother, the wicked mother-in-law, was set on getting his brother re-married so she could have grandchildren. Thinking back, grasping Sanju had suddenly stopped talking about his family problems and whenever I asked him how things were at home, he would hastily answer there were no problems, all was well at home. Furthermore, Sanju once told me he willingly, without any consultation with me, signed over, to his brother his share of his parents' house. I was furious asking why he did not feel the need to talk about it first especially when our own home was heavily mortgaged, and we did not have any savings. He explained it away by saying his brother had a young family needing security and that we were both professionals capable of earning high salaries to support ourselves. That, according to me then, was not a valid explanation but Sanju refused to discuss it any further saying it had nothing to do with me.

Whilst still living in Dartford, I recalled information about the day his mother called with good news about the birth of his nephew. Sanju did not seem interested or pleased, he did not even ask how the mother and son were doing or congratulate his mother. Abruptly putting the phone down, left the room returning ten minutes later when I challenged him about his cold, rude behaviour over the phone towards his mum saying that was not very polite. I congratulated him on the birth of his nephew, but he again walked out of the room. I took that to mean Sanju being the miserable sod that he had become. Another justification was Sanju keeping me out of his family affairs rightly or wrongly that's how it has always been. We spoke no further about it, though normal conversation would be centred around, when he was going to see his nephew, were mother and son back home, both in good health and talk about buying gifts for the baby. Nothing of the sort! It was beginning to add up and top of the list was his refusal to introduce me to his family or talk about them.

Anyway, coming back to my life in Birmingham after Sanju drove off in a huff because I did not show any concerns about his nephew's health issues. I busied myself with work and other social aspects like going to the gym and contacting relatives for a chat. After a week, Sanju called to ask how I was doing. I told him all was well at my end and asked him how he was doing? Sanju was chatty about work and going out with his friends for drinks and a meal telling me that next time I visit

Dartford he will take me to this brilliant restaurant they went to. His chat was beginning to annoy, according to him his life was full of sunshine and partying. interrupted his 'oh so wonderful life talk', to ask after his nephew. He simply went quiet and then I let him have it telling him that it was his child. Sanju started laughing over the phone asking if I had been drinking knowing fully well that I had been a teetotaller for some time. I challenged him saying that it was beginning to make sense especially since he had lost interest in me. Sanju was not having any of it insisting I was sick in my mind; he called me psycho needing help. Said it was disgusting just listening to me mentioning it asking me to call him back when I was in my right mind calling me a lunatic and put the phone down. There was no further communication from Sanju but about a month later he posted me proof of a DNA test result showing that his nephew was not his son. He had taken a sample of both their hairs and sent it for lab testing. I called him to say that I was not convinced. His younger brother was living with his parents, I threatened to pay them a visit to find out the truth for myself. He was adamant I was to do no such thing insisting both his parents were frail, elderly and in poor health. He wanted assurances from him that I would not contact or visit his family in Birmingham whilst he was in Dartford and that he would personally arrange a meeting with them when he next comes over. I knew he was playing for time lying as usual hoping to win me over with his reasoning. Soon became clear to him, I wasn't having any of it, he was becoming agitated over the phone using his usual spiel trying to throw guilt trips saying that noticed how much I had changed from being so loving to becoming hardheaded and said he was beginning to think I had an ulterior motive for causing him heartache. The way he was talking it sounded as if I had the problem and he was right, I had enough of his lies and bull dozing through his virtuousness at my expense. Not this time, he knew I was serious and a visit to his parent's house was imminent. Over the next week, Sanju, endlessly tried to contact me via my mobile phone via emails, even calling my landline number. I ignored his attempts, his relentless tries to pull me into his explanations and assurances. Somehow, expected him to turn up at my door and begging to be heard and not taking no for an answer thus making me nervous and warry of leaving home in case he was outside. The following weekend was unsettling for me as I kept thinking he was going to pay me a visit but nothing of the sort happened. I was glad when the weekend was over assuming he was at work and a long way away in Dartford.

My assumptions were shattered when a couple of days later, unexpectedly, the phone rang seeing an unknown number, I reluctantly answered it and was surprised to hear to be informed that it was Dinesh, Sanju's brother. Dinesh sounded extremely distressed. Being curious and alarmed at his anxious sounding voice, I reluctantly asked him why he was calling. He refused to say anything other than it was important that we meet. He pleaded on the phone for a meeting insisting he was unable to discuss over the phone. The thought did enter my mind that Sanju had put him up to it but that did not make sense given his despair in his voice. I used to know his brother, but after the business folded, we lost touch. He was decent type of person, softly spoken, respectful in his mannerisms, not very tall, slim build, smartly dressed. I did have a soft spot for him, and unlike Sanju, we used to laugh and joke together. No amount of me insisting he tell me over the phone made any difference, he started crying, pleading we meet soon, it was important. Reluctantly, still thinking it may be a conspiracy by Sanju. I agreed to meet him at my local Starbucks later that day. Putting phone down, my mind was bamboozled by all sorts of thoughts rushing into my mind. Has he found out or has Sanju put him up to it to try to quell the rumour? What if it was a set-up or a trap? Should I be going on my own or take someone with me? Then thinking the meeting was in a public place I decided to go it alone and not worry after all he had a problem not me. As time got nearer to our meeting, I couldn't stop becoming nervous, finding myself opening my wardrobe struggling to choose something to wear, smart or casual. Then wear make or go make-up free and trying to apply lipstick my hands were shaking. I sat down in a chair and took some deep breaths to calm myself down thinking this is ridiculous. Why am I feeling like this, am I nervous or fearful of the approaching meeting? Surely, Sanju is not going to be there. What if he turns up and starts hassling me. Maybe not a good idea gong on my own but who can I take with me without sounding alarmist. I will have to tell them about the meeting and Sanju's latest shenanigans and asking his brother to meet with me to try to convince me he was not the father of his children. Then again, why would Sanju share something so sensitive and shameful with his brother? Sanju can do or say anything if it means saving his own skin.

This is a catch 22 situation, if I ask someone to accompany me then I must tell them what it's all about but there again what if it is something else and I was overly thinking. I decided to go it alone promising myself to stay alert and keep my escape route within my eyesight and not be seated somewhere I am unable to get away quickly. Reluctantly, I slipped into a pair of jeans and a jumper grabbing a jacket to wear on top. However, before leaving home I left a message for my son telling him that I was meeting Dinesh in our local Starbucks at 3pm. Leaving home before climbing into my car, I could not help looking around to see if any strange cars were parked close by. As I drove towards Starbucks, I kept glancing at my mirrors suspecting that I was being followed. Though a short drive, it seemed to take ages to get there, every traffic light turned red as I approached. Thought did occur that maybe still time for me to turn round and go back. I felt vulnerable because having accepted the meeting request, I was not sure what was going on around me even as I was driving so best to carry and stop in a safe parking place at Starbucks. Driving into Starbucks car park it looked busy with about ten cars parked on either side. I found a parking space and reversed in thinking about my quick escape. Whilst sitting in the car, I scanned the environment, observing all that was going on outside. There were four teenagers coming out chatting and laughing loudly. I could see a couple of cars parked in the drive-in area waiting to collect their drinks. The area I was parked in seemed quite giving me the confidence to step outside and quickly make my way towards the entrance glancing round to see if I was being followed. By this time, I was very nervous, my heartbeat was fast, I grabbed the heavy door pushing it open, barging in nearly tripping on my own feet. Somehow the door closing behind me brought on a sigh of relief that I had made it safely indoors. I stood there checking the whole area looking for any familiar faces. Inside Starbucks, was packed, noisy but vibrant. Walking towards the service area queuing to place my order and at the same time glancing over my shoulder to make sure all was ok. There were three individuals before me waiting to order, I looked around the room to spot any vacant, suitable seating spaces finding a couple. I was beginning to feel relaxed, looking at the menu board decided to order a regular latte and slice of carrot cake. There were two staff members serving with a third busy tending to the drive-through area. The staff members were trying their best to serve swiftly but the whole process from ordering, paying, making and serving was anything but drawn out.

I noticed a sense of irritation coming into my mind at having to wait longer than I thought, and this caused me to look around at the entrance for any sign of Dinesh. My turn came and I promptly placed my order. The young girl serving me was friendly and had a beautiful smile, I smiled back and asked her if she had been busy to which she answered unusually so today. I paid for my drink, placed the plate with cake on the tray and proceeded to move on to the end of the counter which was busy with some individuals collecting their drinks. I got my regular latte making my way towards the seating area, spotting a round table with seating capacity for three people. I put the tray down, took off my jacket, looked around and sat down facing the entrance taking a sip of my drink nearly burning my tongue as it was piping hot. I admonished myself for not paying attention and eat a piece of cake to reduce the burning effect. Peering around the room, there was quite a mix of people, young, elderly, school kids still in their uniform, three young mums with babies in push chairs happily chatting away. There was an elderly couple sitting opposite silently sipping their drinks looking content with themselves not saying anything, such blissful beingness. Another couple sitting in the far corner of the café, seemed to be all loved-up making me possibly an affair going on. About six students on a long table had plugged their laptops into the available ports, I guessed, studiously doing their homework. Overall, the ambience of this Starbucks is bland with attention paid to keeping it looking rough and rugged, even the seats are uncomfortable. This would not be my choice of place I want to hang around in but was close to my home and its open plan seating provided me with feelings of being safe. Taking further sips of my latte, I checked my phone for any missed calls, there were none? I put my phone back in my handbag resting on my lap and waited, becoming a bit agitated at having to wait. Besides the wait was making me nervous as I was dreading the thought of Sanju appearing. What the hell is going on and why did I agree to come? The suspense of what was about to unfold was unsettling.

I did not have to wait long before Dinesh walked over to where I was seated accompanied by another person. I stretched my neck to check if there was anyone else following behind them, but it was just the two of them. What a relief! I took a deep breath trying to calm my edgy nerves, as both approached the table. Sanju's brother nodded his head and introduced his friend Samir to me. Both sat down and seeing I already had a drink; his friend went off to get drinks for the two of them.

Since I last saw Dinesh, about five years ago, he had changed a lot for one he had piled on some extra pounds and was supporting a beer belly. He looked aged, had grey hairs, going bald at the top and his eyes were baggy with dark circles underneath. He looked troubled, as if he hadn't slept well. Courteously, he asked me how I was, and I replied I was doing fine and in turn asked him how he was? He became fidgety, looking uneasy, placing his clasped hands on the table, he cleared his throat ready to say something just as his friend returned with their drinks. His friend Samir was a chubby, happy looking guy much taller than Dinesh. On sitting down, he fixed his stare on me making me uncomfortable. I looked at Dinesh guessing that both had been sent by Sanju to talk sense into me. I turned my attention towards Dinesh, whose facial expression was intense, looking up at me with his sad eyes, saying it was not good news. Thanking me for coming he proceeded to say that Sanju has done something terrible adding, he came down from Dartford two days ago, whilst he was at work, had a massive row with his parents leaving both distraught. His parents contacted him demanding he return home immediately as there was a serious problem with Sanju's behaviour adding he lashed out at his dad. By the time he arrived home Sanju was gone. He went on to say that Sanju left home hurriedly taking Samina, his wife and the children with him.

I nearly fell off my chair! What! I shouted back at him. Dinesh burst out crying saying Sanju told his parents they were his children, not mine, and he had come down with intention of taking them with him including Samina. He said he did not have a clue about it and was pretty shaken up about losing his family and was still in disbelief at what had happened. His friend put his arm around him trying to console him, but Dinesh was distraught crying in desperation. I looked around to see if his distress had caught attention of those sitting around us but no worries there. Dinesh, taking a deep breath asked me if I had known about it and I said that our relationship had been strained for a long time and was the reason for me leaving Dartford. I told him that I struggled to connect with Sanju's moodiness, adding that I did not like the way he talked to me, belittling me at every opportunity he got.

Dinesh than confessed his wife was having problems conceiving, according to her, and both had undergone regular tests whilst Samina was also having IVF treatment, and so he thought. He added Samina not being able to conceive caused a lot of tension at home with relentless arguments leading to quarrels not only at home but with relatives abroad especially when news broke out that his mother wanted him to divorce Samina and re-marry. This information had become common knowledge spreading like wildfire across their own neighbourhood too. He recalls overhearing one of his neighbours telling his mother she needs to throw Samina out if she doesn't leave on her own will. He said that, unfortunately, as per our Asian culture, a woman is held responsible not the man by that he means it was thought that Samina and not him who was infertile. However, all the tests were proving to be inconclusive indicating there was no reason why Samina could not conceive. He said he was very supportive of his wife and stood by her. In time, they were delighted when Samina became pregnant and overnight was treated like royalty by his family. Samina enjoyed the extra attention paid to her by his parents and others. She pampered herself with new clothes and even bought expensive furniture for the bedroom and asked the spare bedroom to be converted into a nursery for the baby. It was a happy time for the whole family as we looked forward to the birth of our first baby. His mother's health showed a marked improvement, and she started doing more around the house. Everyone in the immediate and extended families treated Samina well and made sure she was rested as she was getting tired easily. The strain of having to tell me his story was making him emotionally upset, and tears welled up in his eyes as he confessed that he adored his wife and the children. He then revealed another secret that shocked me even more than his earlier revelation adding that he was sitting on his bed when he noticed the bedroom carpet was uneven in the corner, so he went across, lifted it and found packets of birth control pills that Samina had hidden but in her haste, forgotten to take them. Painfully grabbing his stomach, he looked up and asked me, "Do you know what that means?" I said a resounding, No! He looked down at the floor, heaving a big sigh, saying that he believed Samina never had problem conceiving but had been deceiving him all the while by pretending.

He continued that the truth was she did not want to become pregnant and must have been having an affair with Sanju much longer than he could imagine.

Whilst he was talking, I could not help but think more lives destroyed because of Sanju's deception, sadly this time it was members of his own family at the receiving end. As and when, if, this news breaks out into their community, his parents' lives will become restricted, even attending their local temple will be out of question. Given their strict upbringing, cultural beliefs and norms, their community will shun both outrightly calling them a disgrace. I was left wondering if his parents were in some way responsible for this mess especially Sanju's mother who should have known better, and I was surprised her womanly instincts did not fore warn her of the deceit that both her son and daughter-in-law were carrying out right under their nose. Also thinking that she was blinkered and probably never thought anything else other than wanting grandchildren and making Samina's life hell. If only I could have been present when Sanju told them, just to see the look on her miserable face. She was one person who never smiled, there was something or other always wrong with her health. At times I got the impression she was an attention seeker, not one to put others before herself, her needs or demands. Every year she spent good three months abroad visiting her family and relatives and on returning complained about her health. Her Husband, Sanju's dad, it helped with household chores and shopping. She spent most of her time sitting in front of the fire complaining about her 'aches and pains' watching television. How did I know all this? Sanju often grumbled about his mother's health problems saying she was becoming an awkward person to deal with. She was old fashioned, stuck in her ways, sat sitting around day in day out lacking any meaningful conversations, making others' lives miserable by that he meant people in his household and his neighbours on both sides. She needed to contribute towards doing the housework including cooking meals. Once when I asked him to tell me why his father was putting up with it? His reply was that you don't know my mother. I was brought back to the here and know by Dinesh voice as he continued speaking adding Sanju, he had noticed that he had a soft spot for his daughter and used to bring her gifts and expensive clothes. Sanju was adamant about which school his daughter should attend and insisted on her attending dance classes including ballet at an early age. Ah! Ballet classes, I interjected, that was because I used to talk about my niece who was of similar age attending dance lessons. Dejectedly maintaining feeling inferior in front of Sanju because of his professional superiority, he was the first person in his family, community, who attended university, achieved an IT qualification, went on to do an MBA at a prestigious University, placing him amongst those earning and demanding higher than expected salaries. Sanju had a played a positive role within our community, was well respected, liked and admired for his posh lifestyle, driving brand new car, wearing smart suits and his gentlemanly behaviour. Overall, he was grateful for his advice, trusting him implicitly. Before he could carry on, I lifted my hand motioning him to stop talking, telling him that Sanju's achievements were all thanks to me and his ability to manipulate and lie to get want he wanted. Acting in certain ways, giving the impression he was confident, fearless but notorious for leaching off others especially me. When he was nervous, he would go into a strop, become moody, abusive all to hide his weaknesses and believe me he had many of those I never let on, I could tell when he was struggling or putting on a show of strength but all the while riding high on my tailcoats adding further that he did not achieve any GCSE passes, let alone the confidence to step out on his own. Sanju ending up working for the world class Manufacturing company and later landing his current job in Dartford was down to me. Updating him those days after our business collapsed, Sanju felt hopeless given his home background, lacking any qualifications or career aspirations.

Every time we met, that was all he selfishly talked about. So, one day whilst having coffee at Nero's, Sanju started bleating on about the sorry state of his life, his 'poor me' saga. Same old lamenting saying he was getting fed up dilly-dallying about his nil to zero career choices and in need of a decent job. We discussed his strengths and weaknesses and talked about his passion of working with electrical type of jobs including installing alarms and security systems at home, for friends, extended family members and some local factories. Sanju said he ideally wanted to move away from home to pursue an IT & Computers degree. To stop Sanju changing his mind and wasting my time, I remember picking up a serviette from the table and writing a pledge on it that went something like, '*I swear hereby that from this day onwards I will religiously pursue a career in I.T. and Computers and will not give up until I have achieved my goals'.* We both signed it, and I kept it as a reminder in case he changes his mind or complains. It worked because apart from a few occasions, Sanju did not falter but diligently followed his career path going from strength to strength. We were both pleased when he got placement at University to complete a degree in Information Technology, sorry don't remember the exact title of his degree. Sanju, at the beginning used to consult with me discussing his course work and keeping me updated but as his circle of new friends grew, he became independent. Soon, though it became a bit troubling when he started talking about this fantastic girl in his group, a foreign student sharing a house with three other students. I knew there was more to it and noticeable when he wanted to borrow my car to drop her off at Birmingham airport. I thought that since she lived over in Yardley area close to the airport, she should get a taxi. Anyway, Sanju insisted on dropping her, so I decided to tag along. Not a good idea but I was going to be a party pooper and spoil their farewell. We drove across the city to pick her up, Sanju asked me to wait in the car, but I followed him in. He introduced me to Angela, she seemed like a nice girl and said she'd heard a lot about me. Really! Anyway, her luggage loaded up in the car, we set off for the airport. Angela was flying back to Africa for her summer holidays. Must admit though a short journey, I sensed unease in Sanju's behaviour because I was chatting away to Angela asking all sorts of questions. We dropped her off at the airport parking lot. Poor Sanju, I am sure he would have gone to the check-in area instead of putting her luggage on a trolley and saying goodbye. On a more serious note, I knew there was more to this friendship than being platonic. When the University commenced in the autumn, one day Sanju phoned on a Saturday morning to say he needed to borrow my car as his 'friends' had planned to go out for the day to Stratford-upon-Avon and he had agreed to drive them there. He promised to be back by six o'clock so we could go out for the evening. When he did not come back and it was past six, I phoned Angela's landline number and one of her house mates answered. When I asked to speak to Sanju, he said he was upstairs with Angela in her bedroom. I was not surprised, as it was not the first time either that he was cheating on me. Of course, when I challenged Sanju about being in her bedroom, he said he went up to check her computer she was having problems with.

I did not believe him and decided not to bother as I had already suffered because of his blundering behaviour. He had no scruples, so what else to expect? Coming back to the current situation:

I shook my head and reminded Dinesh that it was thanks to me he achieved all that he did including landing his current well-paid job adding just by being there for him I helped him build his confidence and interpersonal skills even doing mock interviews with him. He repeated Sanju was well respected within their local community that held him up as shining example to their own children hoping they too would excel. As mentioned before, his brother added that Sanju was seen as being well-educated, smartly dressed in designer clothes, driving a brand-new company car whereas he a lowly taxi driver.

Sanju, fortnightly or once a month according to when I was made aware, drove to Birmingham, stopping on his way to see me, now we know why? I could never understand how someone could drive 200 miles wearing a suit and tie unless it was to impress his family and neighbours. I imagined him driving up his road, parking, getting out, gathering his bags, still wearing his suit and tie, and walking up to his parents' home. Sounds bitchy but then I know Sanju to be a poser! This it seems was the backdrop used by Sanju to gain an upper hand over his backward or semi-literate family. They were in awe of him and his greatness.

As the saying by **William Shakespeare** goes, *some of are born great, some achieve greatness, and some have greatness thrust upon them.*

As for Sanju he achieved greatness, thanks to me, and as a result then had greatness thrust upon him by his family, neighbours, and community in awe of him.

Looking him in the eyes, I asked him if his own mother's behavior by demanding Samina produce a child and talk about you divorcing her, had anything to do with what happened. He confessed at first his thoughts, however he soon changed his mind when he found stash of birth control pills hidden under the bedroom carpet adding that eventually truth would have come out. As to why Sanju suddenly decided to come down or the trigger for his hasty actions was a mystery to him. I am looking at the strain on his face, not having the heart to tell him about my last conversation with Sanju whereby I had threatened to tell his parents about Sanju and Samina's sordid affair taking place right underneath their noses in their home.

Only those two know how long the affairs have been going on and the reason for the betrayal of so many people. What about the children, do they know the truth? His brother is unraveling the truth.

He continues speaking, saying when his daughter was born, both his parents were pleased to have a granddaughter and doted on her. She brought endless joy into their weary lives adding how or when it happened was starting to make sense. Sanju, as already mentioned by me earlier in the story, used to come home once a month usually on a Friday night returning on Sunday. His brother alleged, as a taxi driver, Friday and Saturday nights were his busiest times meaning he did not come home until early hours of the morning. Another thing he added is due to his parents' health problems and his mother's arthritic joints condition, both slept downstairs to save them coming climbing stairs at nighttime because they only had one bathroom that was downstairs. This gave Sanju and Samina the ideal opportunity for their illicit affair. He continued stating that he was not sure when their affair started or what inflamed it. He said, his wife, Samina was a homely type of person not well versed in worldly affairs and only went out with him and that to do shopping or visit relatives.

Suddenly breaking down and crying into the palms of his hand, struggling to speak up, he went on to quietly say after the birth of his second child, his son, he noticed Samina's behaviour towards him began to change but he put it down to her being busy with the newborn. He recalled, his parents had mentioned, they often heard Samina talking to someone on the phone but assumed it was me calling from work. Apologising to me for breaking the terrible news. I told him I had my suspicions but could not put my finger on it until a few days ago adding that I may have been the catalyst that pushed Sanju into action because I had threatened to expose him. I could not even bring myself to say sorry to his brother seeing him so distraught was heart breaking. I had had enough of Sanju and his family sagas in my life, and in a way, was glad I found despite Sanju's best intention to cover up and carry on his vile behaviour by blaming me for being insensitive. Made me physically sick just thinking about him sleeping with his younger brother's wife and brazenly cheating on me.

All this was getting too much for me, I stood up to leave telling his brother to look after himself and walked away. Leaving Starbucks, looking in the mirror smiling, knowing it was time to shut the door on Sanju for once and for all. I did swear out loud and call him some unpleasant names not worth repeating. No sir, not anymore and not wasting any more time on the looser, Sanju.

First thing on returning home, I deleted Sanju from my contacts list, no more wasting time or falling for his 'poor me', sob stories. Determined this time there was no way back for him. Even as a friend. It was time to tell my family the whole truth including

Sanju turning out to be the father of his brother's two children. I also emailed Sanju stating that my family has been told about his abusive behaviour towards me about my meeting with his brother, who told me his wife left home to go and live with him in Dartford. They also knew about him fathering two children with her. I ended my email by asking, 'who is the sick one know'? I told him to get professional help before he does any harm to his new family. I ripped up all photos of his, threw a couple of albums in the rubbish bin, collected his love letters taking great pleasure in burning them, but my hands were trembling with rage as I did so. Any items shared with him or given to me by him over the years were dumped at the local charity shop. Items of clothing he used like to see me wearing ended up the same way.

What impact was all this having on me and my nerves?

I was feeling bitter about the way our relationship ended, struggling to bring about a closure or accept the truth. Admitting that I had borne the brunt of his actions and by walking away let him get away with so much. He had turned my life upside down. Sadly, I did miss him because I was still in love with him and often thought about him walking back into my life. Waiting for the phone to ring or an email or text to come through was downside of not having a proper closure though in front of my family, I pretended things were fine, I was fine and Sanju was history.

Saying, doing and believing are three different things. I had made my bed and now lying in it I was struggling to get a good night's sleep with one question repeating in my mind. Why I let him miss treat me so badly? Was it because I was so in love with him, thinking my love could change him. Surely sooner or later he would have come to his senses and reciprocated my love and sacrifices made to elevate his lifestyle and professional career.

Sanju, took great pleasure railroading over my feelings and emotions and not to mention the financial hardships endured for trusting him. Silly me, all the while I was dismissing his sadistic behaviour believing it must be something I said, did or did not do. He took advantage of my natural, deep-seated characteristics of being loving and caring of wanting to make things better for him.

He used my good nature, confident demeanour by pretending to be needy and one who craved looking after saying no one has ever shown him love or consideration, not even his mother reminding me time and again how she abandoned him at a very young age to spend time in 'India' leaving him with his eldest brother. Often repeating he was not worthy of anyone's love, least of mine as I was so polished, prim and proper. Claiming to be the badass, badly behaved, insecure, struggling to 'belong and feel wanted'.

Of course! I would tell him that I cared about him and say his bad behaviour was down to not being loved and that I would love him to the moon and back. So, I had put myself on a mission to prove to him how much I loved him because if I did not love him, I would not care about him. That explains why time and again I kept forgiving his abusive actions: mental, emotional, physical and financial. I had hard wired myself to only loving him believing that to be a normal in any relationship especially when Sanju talked about us being soul mates, being compatible, being tuned into each other's psyche. By calling me his princess and constantly telling me I was beautiful, intelligent, modern unlike women in his own family or community, was walking into a well laid trap believing him even after he had cheated and defrauded me. Not him, but I was beginning to think there was something wrong with me and I needed to talk to someone, get counselling. He had succeeded in 'character assassination', I was left feeling low, lacking in self-confidence, struggling to breathe through his latest selfish expose.

Slowly, but surely, I was recovering. As the days went by, realising the depth of his deceptions, all in the name of love and loving. How many times I heard him say or use the phrase, 'if you loved me you wouldn't behave like that' or 'how could I not know about his feelings'. He had the Pavlov effect on me, meaning after some time he did have to say anything, just looking at the expressions on his face, I was already jumping up and down wanting to please him.

I was unaware that the balance of our relationship had tilted towards him and his needs, all about him. Thinking back to the time I had my major operation, though he sympathised with me, at the same time he was making demands, some covertly, that I was fulfilling. Like the time when he came over to my place one Monday morning demanding I take money out on my credit card so he could make a payment, he wasn't asking but telling me, marching me to the bank to withdraw funds and handed them over. When we got back home, he was gone like a flash.

I also remembered him telling me that even before we became an item, how he used to drive past my house to catch a glimpse of me adding he nearly got caught once when I was out walking the dog, and he thought I may have seen him. He was stalking me. He told me that long before we got together, he had decided to win me over. On hindsight, looks like Sanju had a game plan he had been working on for some time and unbeknown to me I was his target. It did not happen straight away, but Sanju acted as the gallant cavalier ready to rescue me from a bad relations and upcoming divorce. He had a fetish for my beautiful feet, liking, complimenting the colour of my nail polish. Another action was leaving a red rose on my car dashboard and setting a beautiful romantic song to play on my CD player usually whilst driving home after work in the evenings. Now I see them as entrapments to keep me sweet and thinking of him as a caring lover.

At the start of our relationship, it was alluring getting so much attention and being pampered by him. Meetings after work, going for meals or the movies or going for a walk in the park was romantic. We were like two kids laughing, joking and having fun. Life was sheer joy, and I remember thinking I was the luckiest person on this earth as everything was beautiful not a shade of grey even as cold dark winter days drew closer life was full of fun. I was on cloud cuckoo land. My life it seems had a meaning. I could not wait to wake up in the mornings and get to work to see Sanju. I never though let up on any of my other responsibilities and in fact became a better mother to my sons. I was happy, full of life and all around me noticed the subtle changes in my behaviour and appearance with someone commenting I was beaming with energy. Yes! That was the right word to describe me, beaming. Full of energy, vitality ready to lift away to la la land.

That was then, when I first fell in love with Sanju. When things started to change or rather when did Sanju's mannerism towards me change? It was obvious from the start that Sanju felt uncomfortable around when his family was present. On occasions when either we invited his family or vice versa, he was quieter than normal almost watching everyone talk. I put it down to him feeling uncomfortable about his family not knowing about our relationship. Then there were the warehouses he went to purchase goods from but would not let me accompany him or when I did, asked me to wait in the van. I thought he was being protective of me because the owners and staff were mostly men. But on the flipside when it came to sourcing funds, he would push me forward whether it was to meet bank manager(s), approaching friends, family or even contacting a long-lost college friend. At the start of our relationship, I was financially suave, not in any debt, and that was of great comfort. Soon though, I was running around like a blue housefly trying to find sources to borrow money, assuming that would be the last time. Not if Sanju could help it by throwing his guilt trips at me or going into a panic mode highlighting how much was at stake especially when according to him we had come so far and achieved so much. Alas! I was totally unaware the money was being sucked up into a bottom less pit. Moreover, Sanju's cultural upbringing played an important part whereby being a man he refused to be disrespected and answerable. Safe to safe the words, 'women do as I say and not as I do', resonate with me now. Besides everything around, me was moving at a fast pace including my divorce procedures and problems with my extended family members. Safer to admit, I was struggling to cope, moreover, sudden change in Sanju's attitude towards me of becoming aggressive and demanding, added to the confusion with me thinking it was due to my absence from the business to manage my other affairs. Startling though, as not a pattern of behaviour I had come across before in my life. Although, bewildered by his change in attitude, I put it down to work pressures and having to work seven days. At this point in time, I had no idea or inclination of anything awry going on, including mismanagement of funds.

All I knew or wanted to know was that I was in love with Sanju and him with me!!

I failed to notice, my trust was being abused, he was becoming a control freak, deliberately playing mind games to cause confusion and subvert me. At times trying to convince me that I was a wind-up merchant, making him loose his temper having to apologise for his regrettable outbursts. On hindsight, unbelievable, I put up with so much abuse and bad behaviour hoping we were going through a bad patch, and things would settle down and we would live happily ever after. I so much wanted to believe me were meant for each other.

I was a newbie to the harsh negative elements introduced into my life by Sanju i.e. being abusive, ranting & raving, throwing things about, slamming doors, breaking things and outright selfish behaviours. I bargained for love never expecting such a harsh wake up call. Point being I am still unable to explain to myself why or how I got him so wrong? Perhaps love made me blind.

Back to my life after dumping Sanju and his brother's confessions about his wife's affair and finding out this that his kids were not his.

Having ended my relationship with Sanju meant shutting the doors to his melodramas and getting on with my life. It was easier than anticipated.

Life was getting on peacefully, but Sanju's dramas knew no ending. Read on for his next escapades that once again blew my mind, cost so many lives and in the process nearly cost mine.

12: THE FINALE

Weeks, turned to months and then nearly a year before out of the blue I received another call from his brother. This time he sounded even more frantic than previously. Once again begging me to come to his place immediately. I asked him what was going on, but he kept insisting on me coming over before it's too late. Too late for what I asked. The phone went dead on me, leaving a cold chill up my spine. I could tell by his voice some drama was going on. I quickly dialled 999 and told the operator about the phone call I just had expressing my concerns that it sounded serious. Much to my dismay the operator kept asking me to clarify what I thought was about to happen and why? I tried my best to explain but failed miserably and became frustrated. I gave her his address and begged police be sent round to make sure all was well. Judiciously, the operator asked what I feared was going to happen and I said someone may get hurt and put the phone down.

Grabbing my phone and car keys, I rushed towards my car. Getting in, quickly reversing out of the drive, drove towards their address, desperately trying to keep within the speed limit. I was worried and could not get his dreadful voice out of my head, all the while trying to think what could be happening at his house. Soon found myself turning into his road, approaching the house, I spotted Sanju's car and then saw two police cars with flashing blue lights drive past me coming to a screeching halt outside the house. My heart sank, legs were shaking like jelly, stopping my car a few doors down I watched the policemen rush out of their cars, running towards the entrance and gangway. Slowly stepping out of my car, my legs gave way, grabbing the car door for support me from falling over. Standing up straight and taking a deep breath, shut the car door and walked towards the house. I could hear a lot of commotion, shouting, screaming coming from within the house and noticed the police hadn't gone in but were surrounding the house. Two more police cars came dashing down the road followed by another police van out of which stepped armed police carrying rifles and machine guns. Suddenly someone placed their hand on my shoulder, turning round I was shocked to see a police officer grabbing me pushing me to the ground. As I hit the ground, I saw armed police officers run past me. I was ordered on my feet and told to move right back, no questions asked.

Having been pushed back to where a crowd was beginning to gather, including neighbours from either side of the address who were asked to leave their premises. I desperately tried to listen into conversations taking place between some of the neighbours wanting to find out what was happening. By now, the address was surrounded by police marksmen, there seemed to be a lot of activity going on, but I could not make out what was happening so decided to move across the road to catch a better view. All the lights at the front of the house were on, my attention was drawn to someone moving in the bedroom on first floor than catching a glimpse of Sanju struggling with a woman. He was trying to grab at something she was holding and at the same time moving towards the window. As both moved closer to the window, I saw he had snatched what looked like a baby from her arms. Holding the baby in one arm, with the other arm he was holding Samina in front of him as a shield. I could see him pushing the women towards the window, he or she, not sure as could not see clearly, flipped it wide open it. Within a flash of a moment, Sanju flung the baby out of it with gasps and shouts from the crowd asking him not to. Sanju. Then pulled back and soon appeared again repeating the same stance, holding Samina in front as a shield and dangling his daughter with one arm. He threw his daughter out of the window and then dragged Samina back into the bedroom. Whilst it looked as if we were watching the events unfold before our eyes in slow motion, it was all over within a blink of the eyes. I stood there motionless with my eyes fixated on the bedroom window trying to catch a glimpse of Sanju. The gathered crowd were hysterical, some crying out loud at what they had witnessed. Under protection from the police marksmen some officers dashed towards the children lying still some distance away from each other. I saw the two officers tending to the children, shake their heads it seems due to the impact of them landing on the concrete floor both were dead. In the ensuing commotion, I ran towards the house shouting Sanju's name telling him to stop as I could see he was trying to drag Samina towards the window. Unbeknown to the crowd some officers, had broken down the door and entered the house. When I looked up at the bedroom window, I could see armed police officers aiming their guns at Sanju, ordering him to let Samina go. Sanju was not paying any attention, holding her in front of him making it difficult for them to take aim. I frantically, called out to him again and this time despite the commotion he heard me through the open window. As he turned round to look at me, an armed officer took aim and shot him. Sanju fell backwards, smashing into the window and then another shot was fired before all fell silent. An eerie silence followed the shooting lasting for a few seconds.

Then more shots were fired and screams heard. Next thing I remember is waking up in an ambulance. I could see an officer talking to me but struggled to respond as I was in a state of shock, cold, trembling and muttering something back. The ambulance crew had wrapped a couple of blankets around me, and one was holding a drink in front of me refusing to let go as it was hot, and I was still shaking. Next, I saw Sanju's mum and dad being ushered in. Both in a terrible state, his mum was hysterical, crying loudly, flapping her arms about, and had to be dragged into the ambulance. I noticed there was blood on her clothes as she continued shouting and screaming saying that all was finished, no one had survived. I pulled myself up leaning forwards to ask what happened but pulled back as we had never been on good speaking terms instead curling up on my seat hugging my blankets close to me and hiding my head in them. Next, I heard the ambulance pulling away with three unlikely passengers travelling together, all in a state of shock, brought together by a tragic situation and no one able to comfort or even look at each other. The ambulance with flashing blue lights was taking a long time to get to its destination. Curled up in my seat I was longing for my family to put their arms around me, to make feel safe and secure. I was scared and Sanju's mother's wailing was making a bad situation worse. Apparently, Sanju's father had told the crew that she had underlying serious health problems making them reluctant to medicate her. Now and then Sanju's dad shared a quick glance with me full of fear and trepidation in his eyes. I felt like leaning across to hug him, but my own pain and suffering acted as a barrier and turning away from him I broke down and started crying. I was terrified having seen Sanju throw the children from the upstairs window and then disappearing after being shot. One of the crew member's asked if I wanted to contact a family member, I nodded pointing towards the blankets. My phone along with car keys was in my coat pocket. In my rush after the dreaded phone call, those are the only two items I managed to grab before running out of the front door. Reaching for my phone, still shaking, I tried calling but handed the phone over to the crew member saying it was my son's number. My son answered the phone and was told I was being taken to Russell's Hall Hospital for a check-up as I had fainted and hit my head on the pavement but was not given any details as to what had transpired earlier. As the crew member was speaking to my son, I lifted my arm to my head and became aware of a terrible headache and a bandage around it. I looked at the crew member who was handing my mobile phone back to me and she nodded saying there was an injury to the back of my head. Still looking quizzically at her, she continued saying that I had tried to catch one of the falling children leaning to far back losing my balance, falling backwards hitting my head on the pavement. I looked pensively at her asking about the children. She shook her head indicating none had survived. I withdrew into myself holding my head with both my hands wishing Sanju's mother would shut up as her lamenting was becoming unbearable. Soon we arrived at the hospital, and I remember being stretchered into the hospital.

I woke up in a hospital bed semi-conscious aware of a great deal of activity going on around me. I was drifting in and out of consciousness and was being encouraged to stay awake or to wake up. All I could see was the whiteness of my pillow and bed sheets rest was vague. I remember hearing someone calling saying, mum, wake-up mum it's me but slipped into unconsciousness. I eventually came round opening my eyes to see my family standing round my bed. I tried to get up but was discouraged from doing so. A doctor appeared and started checking me over saying, congratulation's I was out of danger. My family was jubilant individually leaning over to give me a hug and a kiss. I too was pleased to see my sons, brother and sister standing over me. I asked them to tell me what happened and was informed that due to the deep wound at the back of my head, I had to be put into a coma to keep me still and allow for treatment and recovery to take place. I asked, 'how long', and was told two weeks, that jolted me into lifting my head and wanting to sit up. With a nod from the doctor, my pillows were re-positioned so I could comfortably sit up. I felt tears well up inside of me and started crying. My son leaned forward, placing his hand on my arm, said that I had been through a major trauma but now needed to look after myself and with help from the hospital staff, to get better and come home.

He leaned forward saying that we nearly lost you mum, and he is not prepared to do so again. Still confused, I stared at him, hugging him close to me apologising for the trouble, worry and heartache all because of Sanju's selfish behaviour. Leaning forward I asked how Sanju was doing? My son shook his head saying he did not make it. And the others, I insisted on knowing! I was informed that only his mother survived the unfolding tragedy. Apparently, Sanju's father who had travelled in the same ambulance with his mother, died of a massive heart attack a day after the incidence. I asked about his brother and Samina and was told both had also been killed. I was left feeling a sense of numbness at such senseless tragedies. Starting to feel tired because of the sleeping tablets given to keep me subdued, I fell asleep waking up sometime later in a room on my own.

Looking around my room, I could see it was like any other hospital rooms I had visited with one marked difference; the nurses' station was located a few yards away from my hospital door. Lifting myself up slowly, looking outside into the hospital, I could see two nurses busy onto their computers. I sat up feeling thirsty but could not reach the jug that had been paced on a trolley table at the base of the bed. I tried to attract attention of the nurses by calling out to them with my raspy voice, but it was not loud enough. Reluctantly, I reached for the calling cord and gave it a tug expecting someone to come running over. Nothing happened!

Looking across at the nurses' station I saw both the nurses busy inputting data. I was tempted to tug once more when suddenly, a patient's support assistant came barging into my room asking what I wanted. I sheepishly asked for a drink that was promptly handed to me. Taking a sip of the water, I glanced at her name badge that said Naomi. So, I said thank you Naomi for the drink and asked how she was today. She looked at me smiling saying she was fine but run off her feet as one of the support assistants had called in sick leaving them short, staffed grumbling, it was nothing new given the current state of the NHS, their hospital was always short staffed and was becoming more and more dependent on Bank staff to keep it functioning. Still complaining that the overall NHS's budget had been cut year on year, and we are wasting money paying over the top to hire agency staff' who according to her, were fuelling or making the crisis worse. It seems I had opened Pandoras Box for there was no stopping her complaints. She progressed by asking me, 'if you had the opportunity to earn more money doing less hours, would you not be tempted?' I shook my head in agreement somewhat regretting asking how she was? There was no stopping

Naomi, carried on saying the country was in a poor state due to greed and lack of good, competent people saying that I will soon be meeting some of the deadwood running our hospital. I asked her who she was talking about, and she answered that some of the staff members call them the 'clip board brigade' because they walk round with clip boards, ticking off stuff, checking time sheets and complaining about too many hours being booked. I gathered she was referring to the management. Just then a matron entered the room and to my relief, Naomi made a hasty exit. The matron asked me how I was feeling, walking over towards the wall removing the daily chart sheet, closely examining it for a while. She proceeded to tell me they were pleased at the speed of my recovery and are looking to discharging me within next few days. A smile broke across my face thinking of what Naomi had been talking about and reminding myself it wasn't my speedy recovery she was after but my bed for their next patient. I looked at her thinking, I had only just come round and had my first drink, and she is talking about discharging me. I haven't had a chance to speak to 'my' consultant about what happened, the treatment, recovery or any side effects, all she is interested in was of my discharge. I was filled with apprehension at not knowing of the uncertainties and unable to assimilate being discharged so quickly. The matron was thoughtless in saying what she did without a proper consultation keen to dump me on my family to manage my condition(s).

I found myself also getting angry and was about to say something to the matron when a Registrar, (senior, I found out later), entered with his entourage of two junior doctors heading straight towards the daily charts, examining them. I thought to myself, wait for signs of compassion or not, more of the same going to be dished out. He looked up at me and asked how I was feeling? I said that I woke up about half hour ago and had a drink of water. Excellent, he commented, turning to talk to his junior doctors using medical terms to explain the situation, having scribbled some notes on the forms, he addressed the Matron. Walking over to my bed sombre looking, he said that unfortunately, given the seriousness of my situation, he wanted to keep me under observation for a few weeks and assess effectiveness of the medications. Further adding, that my wound was healing slowly, and he was not prepared to take any chances and would need regular x-ray reports to keep on top. I looked at the matron and was forced to tell the consultant what I had just been told.

Impossible! Was his response and looking at the matron he said that maybe she should come and see him later to discuss my case. Giving instructions to her about my medications, the Registrar promptly exited followed by his minions. The matron smiled sheepishly saying she got me mixed with another patient, leaving me thinking either the other person suffered from the same conditions as me or looked the same as me. Reasoning with myself and at the same time feeling sorry for being a burden on the NHS. My trauma and admission to the hospital were not planed. I was relieved to hear the consultant acknowledge my condition and length of stay as that could have been worrying if put under constant pressure of not knowing when I would or could be discharged. I was still unaware of what had happened to me. Suddenly, the aroma of food wafted into my room making me peckish, looking forward to a nice hot meal.

One of the support staff walked in carrying a tray. She came over and slowly helping me to sit up, she propped my pillows helping me lean back. She moved the trolley across the bed adjusting the tray of food asking if I wanted tea or coffee. I looked at the food on the tray, expecting a nice hot meal but was greeted by a sandwich and sweet yogurt. The support staff saw my dismay, apologising, she said meals must be ordered a day before and since I was unable to do so, that is the best they can do. Tongue in cheek I replied, so why did you not wake me up'. I asked if I could have some soup and bread, she said, 'sorry no, we don't have any soup'. Looking at the cold, uninviting food on my tray, I was disappointed, picking up my mobile phone to call my family only to find it had not been charged.

I asked if there was a pay phone and was told one would be wheeled in once lunch had been served. Looking at contents on my tray, I thought, call this lunch, settling for a of cups of tea. Placing my head back on the pillow, I dosed off to sleep. I was woken up by sound of a trolley entering my room. I looked at the phone and then the bringer who was looking at me. I asked her, 'what am I supposed to do with it as it was a pay phone, and I don't have any money on me?' She abruptly replied, 'then you can't use it' and proceeded to wheel it out of my room. I was left gobsmacked thinking my fault for being so stupid or was it their 'we don't give a damn', attitude. Surely, I can't be the only patient waking up penniless and wanting to contact their family? You can't just bring a pay phone and then take it away if a patient has no money. This can't be right, there must be a solution, so I pulled the cord again and when a member of staff came in, I told them what happened.

She assured me to not worry and said if I gave her the phone number, she would call my family and forward my message to which I replied, here's the number and can you please tell them to bring me a hot meal. She looked at me in disbelief and I pointed at the 'meal' in the tray adding that upon waking I was expecting a hot meal not a cold sandwich and yogurt complaining I had only just woken up from a serious operation. She was not happy but took the number and marched out of the room. For God's sake, isn't there anyone without an attitude towards me! Or is there something about me encouraging this type of behaviour? Feeling sorry for myself, I laid back and fell asleep, being woken by someone calling out it was time for my medicine. I turned round to be confronted by a nurse standing squarely in front of me and another one behind her. Gently sitting up, my pillows were straightened up, so was encouraged to use their contour to lift myself up still half asleep. The nurse gave me the medication then proceeded to do other checks, smiling at me saying all was looking good. Ok! I thought what now? She advised me to continue resting. What do you think I was doing before you woke me up and now you want me to go back to sleep like a good little girl. I suppose staff must do their duty and if they were to wait for the right time then nothing would get done. Huffing a bit thinking at least no more disturbances for some time but I was proved wrong. No sooner had I settled down, than it was teatime or was it dinner but at 17:30 it was neither here nor there. I was glad to pull myself up again, sitting up looking eagerly at my next feast about to be served. No! It was another sandwich with ice cream for a desert. I felt like putting my head under the covers and letting out a scream. The staff member reminded me that she hoped I had ordered my meals for the following day. Sheepishly, I shook my head saying I must have slept through when someone came around with the menu. I was told not to worry about it and that she would pick up the menu from the nurse's station. She did that, handing it over she rolled her eyes at me seeing the dinner had not been touched. Under her watchful eyes, I unwrapped my sandwich and took a bite without looking at it. Awwwh! I looked down and noticed I had bitten into a chicken sandwich. I spat the mouthful out pushing the tray away from me explaining I was a vegetarian. When I looked up, saw her disappearing out of the room. Not feeling at all well, frustrated at being served cold, unpalatable, non-veg food, I burst out crying. A nurse entered my room bringing me a cheese sandwich. Though feeling utterly miserable, I was touched by her caring action and thanked her. Having eaten the sandwich, I perused menu filling out my choices.

Thus, life in the hospital flowed between resting, eating, visits from the consultant/nurses, taking medication and eagerly awaiting visits by family and friends. After a week, I was sent for further head MRI scan and informed there was no deep tissue damage and wound was healing but told to expect headaches and slight memory loss problems. I was grateful for the excellent treatment being given to me, feeling secure knowing I was in the right place though struggling due to headaches and painful memories. The blessing for me was being unable to focus on anything thing for too long.

One day, whilst resting in the afternoon, I became aware of someone's presence in my room, opening my eyes, I was stunned to see a familiar looking face, though vague, staring down at me. Pulling myself up sitting straight, I looked earnestly at the person standing before me. I nodded to him, and he nodded back asking how I was feeling. I replied, much better, hoping to be discharged soon adding I was struggling to recognise him ushering to sit down on chair next to me. He replied he was Dinesh's friend. I asked again, who, he said Dinesh's friend and reminding me that we met at Starbucks. He was visiting Sanju's mum and was told I was in the same hospital. I enquired after Dinesh's mother saying I had no idea which ward she was being cared for. I was told she was in a main ward still in shock, giving everyone including staff members a hard time and seems none of her relatives have been to see her and there was a question mark about sending her home to an empty house. The social workers were trying their best to contact her relatives, failing anyone coming forward, including her neighbours, she could end up in a care home. His friend admitted feeling helpless because his own family have forbidden him from brining her home blaming her for the tragedies. I summoned him to the empty seat, as he was still standing by the bed, and sitting down holding his head in his hands, started crying. I reached out to console him, patting him on his shoulder asking him to be brave. He looked up teary eyed weeping Dinesh was his best friend who worked hard to support his own family and parents but never got any proper support or appreciation from any of them, they were all selfish. Dinesh was expected to be the perfect son and husband but when truth came out it hit him hard, he was struggling to cope, could not make sense of the situations and worse still got no support from his parents, especially his mother, who whinged and whined about being shamed in the community. Not once did she put her arms round Dinesh to comfort him. Had it been Sanju, her favourite one, she would have been all over him like a rash. Dinesh was a broken man, feeling lonely and isolated but when Samina called him asking for help, he was quick to respond as he feared for their safety.

What do you mean, I asked him.

He told me after moving to Dartford to live a happy family dream with Sanju, things turned nasty when Samina overheard Sanju chatting to a women confessing his undying love for her. When Samina confronted Sanju, he was not prepared to talk about it and over the next few weeks became abusive towards her and the children. Samina realised she had made a mistake moving in with Sanju, begging Dinesh for forgiveness and asking to come home. He continued that one-day Sanju came back home in a foul mood and started shouting at the children. When Samina remonstrated, he hit her hard sending her flying across the room hitting her head on a glass table. She had a cut on the side of her face and bleeding. She begged Sanju to take her to the hospital. Sanju, though convinced her cut was not that bad and that it was not a good move because if police get involved, they will call social service who would take '_her_' children away. Samina managed to stem the bleeding and for the sake of her children went along with Sanju's suggestions. She realised the danger she and the children were in. Next day when Sanju was at work, she placed a frantic call to Dinesh begging him to save them. Dinesh was concerned and told Samina she needs to be careful including deleting her call register and advising her to call 999 at first sign of any threats to her or the children. In the meantime, he was making plans to travel to Dartford to rescue them. So, on Thursday before the incident, Dinesh drove down to Dartford and whilst Sanju was at work, packed as much of their stuff into the borrowed estate car and drove back to Birmingham. He was shocked when Samina opened the door as she was looking pale, had dark circles under her eyes, and was edgy speaking hastily.

Dinesh had not mentioned anything about Samina's phone calls or his intention of travelling to Dartford to bring them back. When he pulled up outside his home with them, his eldest daughter ran into the house arms stretched out wanting to hug her grandparents. Dinesh's mother wasn't having any of it, pushing her granddaughter away. The ensuing drama was not what Dinesh had envisioned, and it was not pleasant. Though, Dinesh had forgiven his wife because he still loved her and the children, his mother was not prepared to have them in the house, shouting and swearing, calling Samina every bad name under the sun, then demanding she and the children be removed from her house immediately. Dinesh begged they be allowed to stay until he can find another safe place for them but his mother's ranting and raving at both meant he could not get a word in edge way. His mother whilst laying all the blame with Samina failed to mention her older son's involvement in the sorry debacle. She was totally in denial about it and went on at Samina as if she had run off with a stranger. Dinesh took 'his' family upstairs leaving shortly to get some essentials for them telling Samina to stay in the bedroom and keep it locked until he gets back and that is how they managed with Dinesh making sure his family had all they needed, and the bedroom had an ensuite so there was no need to use the bathroom on the landing. Dinesh, in the meantime, as well as working, was desperately trying to find a rental place for 'his' family fully aware that his mother could not be trusted as she kept giving him dagger looks every time he came home and moved about the house.

Moreover, when Sanju came back from work and realised they were gone, he immediately phoned his parents' home only for his mother to answer and tell all. It seems Sanju was raging with anger and promised to break Samina's legs for her betrayal. Unbeknownst to Dinesh that Sanju had called, and his mother had spoken to him demanding Samina be removed from her house. Though aware, that Sanju would be making his move, Dinesh was hoping he would have moved them to a safe house before Sanju comes down from Dartford, thinking he may not. Dinesh had stopped working spending as much time with 'his' family and only went out to look for a house to rent. He was caught unaware about his mother's active role in keeping Sanju updated and when he came down from Dartford, he was watching the house waiting for Dinesh to leave or a phone call from his mother informing him all was clear.

Unfortunately, when he let himself in, he was faced with Samina preparing a feed for the baby. Though why she came down, is a mystery or was it a cunning trick by his mother that made her drop guard. Samina, tried to run back upstairs but he grabbed her and started hitting and pushing her around. Hearing the commotion going on in the kitchen, his mother came in and immediately blocked Samina's escape route. She incited Sanju by saying horrible, nasty things about her daughter-in-law, calling her a whore claiming she had been sleeping with other men. The neighbours had seen Sanju walking towards their communal alleyway and knew there would be trouble and upon hearing Samina's cries for help came rushing over but had the door slammed in their faces. Just then Dinesh retuned and was appraised about the situation by his neighbours but instead of entering from the side entrance he made his way to the front using his key to enter and went straight towards the kitchen. He forced the kitchen door open as his mother was standing in front of it holding on to the handle. With help from his father both managed to fling the door open, on entering entered the kitchen found Sanju kicking and punching Samina lying on the floor. Dinesh looked around for something to hit Sanju with and grabbing a knife he lunged towards Sanju who immediately moved out of the way pushing Samina forwards who he had grabbed off the floor. Samina was pushed straight into the knife catching her in the stomach, though wounded, she ran out of the kitchen making her way upstairs to protect her children. Sanju tried to follow her, but Dinesh tackled him to the ground, and both wrestled each other laying punches and smashing into the Kitchen units. Sanju saw the knife on the floor and amongst his parents' shouting and screaming, plunged the knife into Dinesh who fell to the floor and lay still. Dinesh was lifeless, his parents opened the door and ran outside screaming for help. Their neighbours had already phoned the police who started to arrive same time as I pulled up after frantic phone call from Dinesh informing me Sanju was in the house attacking Samina.

What happened after that was all that I was party to. I too was beginning to well up, looking at his friend's face contorted with pain as he continued talking about the incident. Every now and then heaving a sigh saying, I miss Dinesh so much, he was such a gentle, loving person. He did not deserve to die like that. He was protecting 'his' family unlike that monster.

I remarked, 'what a waste of beautiful souls, especially the children'. I did not know Samina well but found myself profoundly moved at her loss of life, and Dinesh, he was an innocent bystander dragged into this sorry saga. Dinesh's friend stood up to leave, looked at me and said he was sorry for my suffering adding that Dinesh thought very highly of me and talked kindly about me mentioning how intelligent and stylish I was. He was grateful for the break I gave to Sanju during our business ventures and afterwards supporting him up his career and work ladders.

As he was walking out of the room, he turned round saying, 'take care' to which I replied, 'you too'. As he exited, my room fell quiet, there was a deep sense of sadness in the atmosphere. Full of remorse, I put my head down on the pillows then rising to pull the cord. I needed medication as my head was pounding with pain, I was traumatised after our conversation and the recollections. Having taken the medication, I soon fell asleep.

Next day, the thought of Sanju's mother being in the same hospital came to my mind and as if by magic, I looked up and there she was standing in front of me looking her usual miserable self. She was accompanied by one of the nurses holding on to her arm. Forever the needy, I thought. I could feel anger build up inside of me, looking at the nurse I pleaded she be removed from my room. Sanju's mother was about to say something, but I motioned her to stop, pointing to the door signalling she leave. The longer she was standing there, the more agitated I was becoming until I shouted for her to leave. The nurse accompanying her was shocked at my response seeing her and walked her out of the room. I was livid at the audacity of this women, who never had time for anyone but herself and now she dared to speak to me. Given my mannerism towards Sanju's mother, it was clear I too held her responsible for the tragedy. I spent rest of the day flinching unable to relax.

I decided to phone my son desperate to hear my loved one's voice as the whole saga had destabilised me to the point of struggling to cope and last thing, I wanted was to deal with such an unsavoury, selfish character. Something about his mother's appearance was troubling me, but I could not fathom the reason for my feelings. I knew something was not as it seemed but what?

After a month's stay in hospital, I was discharged home to continue with my recovery. Whilst the thought of being discharged was good news, I was apprehensive at being on my own as my son was working and had to go away on business matters. However, coming home was not as scary as I had envisioned given, I was still not well and feeling tired most of the time meant I could not do much around the place. Within a week of being at home, I started having flashbacks during the day and terrifying dreams at night. The flashbacks were around Sanju when he turned round, eyes full of rage, before throwing the children out of the window. I had never come across so much hatred and spiteful actions as Sanju's and struggled to come to terms. My nightmares related to trying to save the two children grasping my hands as we are trying to escape from some dark force pursuing us. Finding a safe place, we sit down to catch our breath before a hand appears, grabs both children flinging them into the air. I desperately run towards them hoping to catch them, but both disappear into thin air leaving me hysterical calling after them only to be woken by my son reassuring me it was a bad dream. Sanju living or now dead, continues to torment me. I became a nervous wreck suffering a mental health breakdown resulting in me being referred for medical treatment and counselling sessions at our local mental health centre. These sessions continued for over a year gradually helping me to face the horrors of my life after Sanju, eventually coming to terms with it. Though painful at times, my perseverance and my counsellor's expertise helped me rebuild my life.

I started attending art classes and to my delight discovered I was a natural at drawing and painting.

Have my saga with Sanju come to an end. Decide for yourself as the next chapter unfolds more truths.

13: AN UNEXPECTED MEETING – THE MASK SLIPS

(Finally found out Sanju's true nature and name)

It has been nearly two years since the tragic situation with Sanju and his family whereby all accept his mother lost their lives. Sanju's father, as you may recall, died of a massive heart attack the very next day after the incident.

On a sunny August, I decided to take a trip into Birmingham City centre treating myself to some new clothes and a pair of shoes. Looking pleased at my purchases and feeling peckish, I decided to visit Debenhams Restaurant on the fourth floor for some coffee and sandwich. Travelling up on the escalator, I was keenly looking at the clothes display to spot anything of interest reminding myself that I need to visit their Fragrance Department for some Perfume. I wanted to purchase Estee Lauder Sensuous and ask for free samples. Arriving at the restaurant, I was met by a queue of six people before me. That was fine by me as I was having a relaxing day and was not in any hurry. Whilst waiting to be served, I could not help eyeing their cakes selection tempted to step out to select one. I resisted the temptation sticking to my place in the shorter queue instead focusing on the overhead menu and decided vegetable soup of the day and coffee sounded appetising. My eyes again wondered over to the cakes section and this time apologising to person behind me, I went over and selected a slice of carrot cake. Boring! You must be thinking but it looked so welcoming. Having secured slice of cake on my tray, I cast my eyes over the restaurant floor to find an empty place. Having purchased my food and drink, I walked towards my target location but instead of stopping there, decided to continue towards an empty seat by the window. I sat down and started to enjoy my feast. It was as I was washing it down with sips of my hot coffee delivered by the waitress, that I noticed someone walking towards me. This time I recognised him, and he was Dinesh's friend. He walked over beaming a smile at me. As he approached the table, I stood up to shake his hand asking him how he had been keeping. He said he was fine and commented at how well I was looking. I thanked him asking him if he wanted to join me for a coffee. He agreed asking if I could do with another drink. I shook my head and asked for normal coffee. Dinesh's friend returned with the drinks and another slice of cake offering it to me. I pointed to the empty crockery dishes on the tray besides me saying I have already been fed. Dinesh's friend sat down, and we talked about everyday happenings. Then I looked at him asking if he has recovered loss of his friend. He replied that not a day goes by when he does not think about him adding they had been childhood friend. Reluctantly, I asked after Sanju's mother. His reply that she was with her older son and daughter-in-law shocked me as Sanju had never mentioned them and given the impression Dinesh was his only sibling. Dinesh's friend saw the look of surprise on my face before continuing to add that his brother and sister-in-law were traced by the police and arrived on the scene taking full control of all the assets belonging to their dad, Sanju and Dinesh claiming to be the rightful heirs. He went on to say whist they were ready to take possession of the assets, they are not happy having their mother live with them and have been trying to offload her into a care home but so far, she has threatened to seize control of the family assets if they tried to get rid of her. From what I was hearing it was not a pleasant situation and one I was not interested in or willing to sit here and feel sorry for her. Desperate to change the topic, I asked him his name and was told it was Aslam. I smiled and said it was nice knowing his name. He looked sternly at me saying he was glad that we met as there was something he needs to tell me. I waited patiently as Aslam looked around him, then out of the window and started to get up to leave. I asked him to sit back down and tell me. He blurted out that Sanju was not Hindu but Muslim.

Sanju was not Hindu but Muslim, I exclaimed!

Yes! He added it was a ruse he carried out to deceive you because he knew you would not have fallen for him or gone into business with him. He said Dinesh did not want to be part of this ploy, but Sanju threatened to beat him up if he ever opened his mouth. He said Sanju had been violent towards his whole family who lived in fear of him including his parents, adding his mother was the one to embolden his devious ways as she never instilled any virtues into him but always treated Dinesh badly calling him all sorts of dehumanising names.

I repeated, Sanju was a Muslim! How come I did not pick up anything? What was his real name?

Aslam said Sanju's real name was Shahid Ali, Dinesh's was Altaf!

I slumped back into my seat spell bound by the news thinking how that could be possible. I looked up and said that I moved in with the guy. But no sooner these words came out of my mouth, I regretted saying them thinking I was part of this deception. I looked up at the ceiling shaking my head than stared at Aslam saying is there anything else I need to know. He shook his head. I thanked Aslam for having the courage of speaking up confirming that I have no hard feelings towards him. He stood up and left leaving me to deal with the shocking truth of my past. I was determined to sit there and think things through and not go home with any baggage.

Sanju being a Muslim was of no concern but the lies he spun to keep his religion a secret was gut wrenching. Sitting there my thoughts went back to his mother and recalled being troubled by her appearance when she visited me in the hospital. It was the way she wrapped the long scarf we call chuni round her head and tucked it behind her ears. This was typical of Muslim women especially the older generation and whilst preparing for prayers.

At this stage, I was not prepared to address what difference it would have made to forming a relationship had he told me he was a Muslim. It sufficed me to know it mattered to him, it was his decision not mine, his pre-planned thinking to carry out the deceit. I was not going to take any blame or minimise his part in the whole affair.

I sat there on my own sometimes staring out of the window or looking straight ahead wanting to think things through. Only one question kept coming to mind and that was, 'how could he?'

Holding my head with one hand, I tried thinking of any signs I may have missed after all we had been together for so many years. I fell in love with him, he was totally besotted with me or was he pretending to be. Then we went into business together as partners. Alas! I realised that was not true because he refused talks of putting legal framework around it meaning signing a contract. He was adamant that was not going to happen because we were a couple, and trust was important. Me going on about it meant I did not trust him. What a fool I have been?

What about the property in Dartford? Wrong again as it was in his name and being a new build all we had to do was visit a show home and then chose the plot for the building. He got the mortgage in his name so signed the papers. Come to think of it, I never did see any formal documents or anything to do with the house, not even telephone or utility bills. He kept them all, but they should have been delivered to 'our' home address. There too I drew a blank and scratching my head for answers trying to remember picking up the post. No nothing, drew a blank. When I moved to Dartford, I was desperate to get a job and that was my prime focus and when I had secured work, I was leaving early and returning home late. Weekends were spent cleaning, cooking and shopping with him holding the purse strings and filling the trolley. Only when I started working and contributing £1700 pounds a month was I able to pick items. I sat there thinking about the time we went shopping to furnish our new home, how disruptive or moody he used to be and remembering an incidence within the BHS household lighting section, he was obnoxious towards me, making me cry. No sooner had I burst into tears then he was all over me apologising and wanting to make-up. Thinking back, I recall him saying that I should stop winding him up. I had become used to putting up and shutting up especially when he was moody to avoid a confrontational situation, whether indoors or outside. No matter what, he would proportion blame at me. I remember leaving home once on a Saturday when he was already being stroppy, walking behind him and looking at the back of his head, I thought to myself he is the devil's re-incarnate. I sensed a negative aura around him. If only I had taken heed. When he forgot his mobile phone at home and I could hear it ringing, before I got to it stopped but I could not access it due to it being locked.

Feeling thirsty, I decided to purchase another cup of coffee and made my way back to the same seat. I glanced around me to catch any action going on within the restaurant area, but all seemed quite with only a handful of customers either sitting on their own or chatting away happily with another. Ah! Happiness! Thinking about my nature, always happy, full of life, smiling and laughing no matter what was going on in my life or around me. I thought it my life's mission to keep everyone, especially my loved ones happy, positive, telling them nothing was worth getting upset about. Using this approach with Sanju (Aslam), was the worst thing I did because there was nothing that would cheer him up, he was miserable as hell, sapping my energies instead, before long bringing me down feeling negative and tired. Same way as

Sanju (Aslam), was miserable by nature, I was the opposite of him, but you've guessed whose behaviour ruled the roost.

Sipping my coffee, it seemed I was determined to think things through as if wanting a closure before going home and wanting to empty my mind of all rogue thoughts about him.

My thought process continued thus! Having moved to Dartford, secured a reasonably paid job and looking forward to settling down, one day I approached him with suggestions of opening a joint Bank account. No sooner had I suggested, he shot it down saying he was not interested and waked out. This was one of those situations whereby, he was able to immediately flatten my prospective thinking leaving me deflated as if someone had let the air out of a football. All I could do was sit there stunned. Thinking back, I tried to recall how on earth I was able to transfer monies into his account without having his bank details, name etc. Surely, it would have shown his real name but trying to remember drew a blank.

What about his neighbours in Dartford? What name did they call him by?

When I moved there, it was the first thing I did was to introduce myself to them. One of the guys he used to play cricket with was a young Indian guy working for Pfizer living with his young family a few blocks away from us. I had asked that he invite them over for lunch but he never it but as luck would have it, once when we were both tidying the front garden, he was out walking with his family and stopped for a chat. I was really pleased to see them but Sanju (Aslam), quickly walked across saying he was too busy and unable to stop for a chat. The guy carried on walking leaving me to think, this guy is not going to be coming round.

Our next-door neighbour, a carpenter, came over to build an extension wardrobe in the main bedroom and whilst he was working, I stood there talking to him about his job and mine. We were engaged in a friendly chat when Sanju (Aslam), walked in rudely interrupting asking how the extension was going on, completely cutting me out of the conversation and then ordering me to make coffee for them. That too was a sad moment for me, I felt insulted, demeaned, in front of the neighbour.

Once when my youngest son came to visit with his girlfriend, we decided to take them into Dartford city to show them some of its UNESCO world heritage sites, museums, art galleries, castle, abbey, cathedral and Dartford Tales. Whilst walking round, Sanju (Aslam), whispered that we just missed his manager and his family. I turned to look back, but they were gone. I got the feeling; he did not want to introduce us to him, but question raised in my mind was how did he avoid them?

Whilst sitting in the restaurant had someone been watching me, they would have noticed me shaking my head again and again. The reminders pouring into my mind held me in disbelief. As I rose to leave, few more thoughts popped into my head. Sanju (Aslam), had attended services with me at our local temple and I was grateful for his commitment as he followed me round bowing before the deities and accepting offering of Prasad, blessed fruits, from the Pandit. Another thought was around him enjoying 'non halal' meet burgers at Macdonald's and KFC, though I do not recall him consuming or purchasing pork or ham.

I left Debenhams restaurant in total disbelief at the latest revelations about Sanju not being Sanju but Aslam, a Muslim and the myriads of examples, thoughts that followed this revelation. I admitted to myself, he was a master of deceit, only a devil can do a devil's work.

14: LOVER'S LOVE LOST - MAKING SENSE

Sanju's aka Aslam, latest revelation did have an adverse impact on me.

'Who better to tell where the shoe pinches than the wearer'

Thoughts of being taken for a ride not once but many times over was another aspect of our relationship I was left to deal with without him. One thing was clear that I was not innocent in this affair in fact by ignoring various warnings and gut feelings, I allowed the pain and suffering to carry on longer than it should have and who knows I could have flushed him out sooner.

Mistakes are inevitable in any relationship but not to the extent involved in mine.

The question is why I put up with so much and not pick-up the signs that something was not right. Sanju acting as an Indian or rather of Hindu religion but being a Muslim who attended Mosque and celebrated EID. To safeguard my own sanity, to not have another breakdown or having to commit to further counselling whereby I must repeat whole episodes of my relationship, I decided to go it alone and explore it myself.

What was it about me that blinded me to his deceptions and when I knew, I still chose to ignore them.

One of the key problems was that not many people liked him including members of my own extended family and it seems the more I was being cautioned the more I wanted to prove them wrong. Sanju, had already told him how much his own family hurt him and that from a very young age he felt no one loved him or cared enough to ask after him. Nicely laid emotional traps, that I walked straight into determined to prove to him that I was different.

Next, I investigated all that was going on in my own life at the time Sanju decided to impress upon me not forgetting that unbeknownst to me he had been stalking me.

I was going through a divorce, working part-time, looking for full-time job or business venture to support my young family and being hassled by my own extended family, relatives and friends. Our family friends deserted me choosing to either not get involved or showed allegiance to the other side. Remember, being an Indian, I was seen as the problem and all the evidence to the contrary was ignored or seen as nothing major to result in a divorce. There is something about our Indian mentality that expects a woman to grin and bear it for the sake of the family honour and respect within the community. I was doing neither, so had to be ostracised, ignored and if that was not enough my ex-husband was supported and given insider information to embolden him even more. My own mother and sisters were complicit in seeing me suffer whilst entertaining him even providing a roof over his head and scheming to remove the roof over our heads.

The divorce agreement made him responsible for mortgage re-payments and I paid the bills, provided for my sons and maintained the house. Soon after the divorce settlement, our house was repossessed, and we were literally made homeless. This was my first problem that I did nothing about meaning did not go back to the court or my solicitor. Why? I can only imagine it was because of the mountain of problems I was already dealing with and not forgetting Sanju had already made his entrance, gone into partnership with him and was struggling to make sense of his changed behaviour towards me. Second problem identified is that Sanju having wormed his way into my life had tactically positioned himself into a place of least resistance. In plain English, my goose was already cooked so when he started abusing me, I had no way out.

This is my truth; I was determined to support my family; I was equally determined to prove the naysayers about Sanju wrong and my own nature of only seeing the good in others was blinding me to his reality. Working six days and then being told to work Sundays by Sanju left me with little time to think. Not wanting to go on bleating about poor me, remember I was suffering ill health and had a major operation when Sanju took over the business and started making demands for cash. There was no one I could turn to, I was feeling isolated as so many doors had been slammed in my face. From the start of my divorce proceedings, I was a pariah, being pushed in all directions but never letting go of my biggest treasure, my sons. Was this another reason why I put up with so much at the beginning but then lost my footing?

15: RELATIONSHIP (LEADING) TO NOWHERE

(Sanju aka Aslam belonged to a dysfunctional family)

As more and more details became known about Sanju's family, I was left in no doubt that his was a dysfunctional family. He told me once that his father's advice to him was if you tell a lie don't back down, persist with it as if it were a badge of honour. His mother abandoned (his words) him at a very young age leaving him at the mercy of relatives to provide for him. Sanju, as I see it now did not know or want to know the difference between right or wrong. His mentality was I want it, and I will have it. How else could he live a Jekyll and Hyde type of life and did it so well.

The mother of many lies as spun by Sanju.

Sanju, confessed at a later stage during our relationship that he used to stalk me, driving past my house in the evenings and at weekends but whenever he spotted me, he would hide or drive away. My worst nightmare was still to come, having covertly planned and played the courting game, he managed to attract my attention and before long he convinced me about being the nice guy, by being polite, gentlemanly, pretending to be coy, ready and willing with his suggestions, showing care and concerns for me, overly complementing me about my looks and intelligence and best of all claiming to never having met anyone like me. I gradually found myself falling for this gentle and loving persona, agreeing to meet him for lunch after work at the Post-Office where I am working part-time.

This was to be our first date! The day came, before leaving home that morning I made sure I dressed smart and throughout the morning whilst working flitted about from being excited to nervous. I finished work came outside hoping in anticipation of seeing him waiting for me. There was no sign of my dashing romantic who had swept me off my feet into a land of daydreaming, soft music and broken down all barriers of shame and respectful conduct. I waited and waited, walked up the street, round the corner, crossed over to see if he had parked by the school to be discreet. Having waited for over an hour and with no chance of contacting him, I got a bus home feeling disappointed. There was no contact from Sanju that evening, but I assured myself of seeing him at the market the next day where he had a stall. Next day, I eagerly entered the market yearning to catch sight of Sanju but instead saw his brother–in-law opening his stall.

All day long I could not summon the courage to ask about Sanju and the curt smile on his face told me he was taking pleasure in my suffering. He never mentioned anything about Sanju and when Saturday came, busiest day of the week, someone else came to open and run his stall. I never heard from Sanju either and his family, who I was sure had become aware of our relationship, they took great pride in coming over to talk to me, but not a word about Sanju.

This went on for over six months and the longer Sanju was absent the more I found myself missing him. As the saying goes, absence makes the heart grow fonder. Our separation happened on our first date. Then out of the blue, my home phone rang and when I answered, it was Sanju. As I was at home and not wanting to raise any suspicions our chat was formal but when I saw him next day, he came over with a big smile and first words that came out his mouth were that I had put on weight. Not nice at all, I was furious but smiled at him asking where he had been. He asked to see me after work to talk about it and I agreed. I must admit, I was happy to see him and wanted to throw my arms around him and give him a big hug, maybe later, in private, I thought!

So where had Sanju been for the last six months? He told me he was in India (but now we know he was in Pakistan) tending to a serious family problem. He profusely apologised for not being in touch claiming it was not possible. I was glad to have him back accepting all that he was saying and besides I had fallen head over heels in love with him. Sanju showered me with a lot of loving attention, presents and flowers literally sweeping me off the floor wanting to make up for the lost time. As if!

Since Sanju's return, his family and mine were becoming aware of our relationship and decided to put a damper on it. His mother claimed that whilst he was away, (in Pakistan), he had become engaged. Alarm bells should already be ringing but I was so in love that when I confronted Sanju about it, he confessed it was a childhood commitment between the parents, and he broke off the engagement. I so wanted to believe him as this type of practice was common in Indian culture. Our love and antics were there for all to see, we were the happiest couple on this planet full of merriment.

Then one Saturday, when Sanju was away from the market one of his relatives turned up to open his stall instead but kept staring in my direction making me feel uncomfortable. Later that day he decided to come over for a chat with another of Sanju's relatives in tow. The conversation soon changed to talking about Sanju. I got the impression both were keen to say something and when I mentioned how well Sanju had done since his return from India (Pakistan), both exchanged looks and then one blurted out he had not gone abroad but was in Prison.

Sanju in Prison for six months, not holidaying in India (or Pakistan)!

They then proceeded to tell me truth about what happened. Apparently, Sanju with two of his mates had broken into a safe of their local Petrol Station where one of them worked and was finally caught when one spilled the beans. On the day of our first date whilst I was left in nervous disposition waiting for him, Sanju was facing a magistrate of law in court for the robbery and was sentenced to six months in prison. Locked up for his role in the crime, he was a criminal! I was shocked of what I was being told.

So how did Sanju wiggle his way out of this latest episode?

When I confronted Sanju, said the real reason for not telling me the truth was due to fear of losing me, someone he had come to love dearly adding that I was the best thing that happened to him in a long time. He claimed to have called me from the prison to confess but every time he heard my voice on the other end, he panicked putting the phone down. Sanju, cleverly turned the situation round on to me claiming he felt I would not understand his situation and leave him. He maintained that, as had been proven by his family members ganging up on him, by talking behind his back about his prison sentence, they were trying to draw a wedge between us, just as he has dreaded and reason for not telling me but suffering it all on his own. In a nutshell it was his family's and my fault for not giving the poor guy a break.

Silly, stupid me, by now already head over heels in love with him, wanting to prove my love was true and keen on protecting him from the vultures circling around 'us', who he claimed were jealous of our relationship and business partnership.

As the saying goes, 'Oh what tangled webs we weave?'

I did not need to weave any webs, Sanju was the master weaver

I ask of myself, 'Pray what is/ was it about you that made me a willing 'prey?'

16: ME A WILLING PREY– HOW SO?

Below quotes go a long way to describe what was happening in my life with Sanju, aka Aslam, not from India but Pakistan

> *"Frailty thy name is woman"* (Shakespeare)
>
> *"Without vanity, without coquetry, without curiosity, in a word, without the fall. Women would not be women. Much of her grace is in her fragility"* (Victor Hugo)
>
> *"What a grand thing, to be loved! What a grander thing still, to love!"* (Victor Hugo)

I was on a mission to save Sanju, to prove to him that not everyone was like the people he had come across especially his own family members who he had claimed had let him down. His father was lacking in morality instilling in his son it was ok to lie. His mother could not think past her own wants needs and desires to be able to care for the children she brought into this world. Conversely, I, Shruti, belonged to a very loving and caring family. My father worked long hours, including weekends but always made time to sit down with me to chat. Though friendly and approachable, he insisted that his children lead balanced lives. My mother was a typical Indian housewife who never went to work and never complained about being 'stuck at home'. She was a homely person enjoying her blessed family, happy to cook and see to other household chores. Because my, parents did not swear or abuse each other or us, I grew up thinking that was the norm. Even when we had a party with relatives and friends gathering, it was a merry time with a lot of dancing, singing but no alcohol. I grew up a vegetarian so never felt the need for a McDonald's or KFC. As a family we would sit together and watch TV and especially around Christmas planned our mealtimes around programmes we could watch.

I was content being part of a caring family, but things changed when my dad passed away and mum went to live with one of my brother's. Our closely knit family fabric that mum and dad had built became fractured as we got older and went on to live own lives. This left a hole in my heart whereby I longed to love and be loved as my parents did.

I was therefore brought up in a loving, sharing, giving environment

Sanju was the wanting, the needy person, I was out to save, to protect him. I could not understand why or how his family had ignored him and his needs and so I thought at the time. I seriously misread the situation though given many signs or warnings that something was not kosher, I chose to ignore them thinking and believing by loving him and being 'nice' to him, I was helping him to be a better person and tidy-up his rough edges namely his anger, swearing and abusive behaviour. I reasoned that he was not used to so much attention and loving environment and he played on that by comparing it to his own upbringing. I believed what I was doing was right and took on the role acting as his father, mother, sister, nurse, teacher, counsellor and advisor amongst other things, not forgetting I was bank rolling him and his demands too.

At the time, I had not realised that by helping, so I thought, Sanju meant, I was giving away more and more control of myself and my freedom. When we first met Sanju had remarked at my independence and wished more Indian women were like me but as our relationship moved forward, he started to put me down blaming me for being modern and not 'Indian' material. I wanted to convince him that was not the case.

Next Sanju disapproved of me wearing short skirts (Sorry! Skirts period) and I stopped wearing them and started covering myself up more cutting back on open blouse collars and T-shirts. He was moulding me without me realising it and I thought it was because he loved me. Sanju had become articulate at explaining away anything and everything and when he was abusive convinced me it was my fault.

I only knew how to love! Getting angry, swearing or being abusive was like a whole new language that I did not understand. The only thing I knew was that it was not nice and when Sanju got angry or abuse, I responded by being nice to him accepting his explanations. I knew what he was doing was wrong, but I believed I could change him instead he slowly and gradually was eating away at my self-esteem and confidence like a blood sucking vampire wanting more and more of my conformance.

As time went on all that loving feeling was submerged under his onslaughts and I began to see the light. My life was entwined with his financially, materially, emotionally and culturally. Remember, I was on a mission to prove to him that I was a good Indian woman for him nothing short of being subservient was acceptable.

I stand by the three quotes listed at the start of this chapter as each played their part in my downfall and his deceit.

Sanju and his family are dead, nothing more left to write about.

This chapter of my life is now closed. Seems Sanju aka Aslam had the last laugh at my expense.

Sanju aka Aslam RIP

Next: Unexpected meeting with Paul, the NHS Consultant at the Outpatient's department. The guy I had a near miss accident in M&S car park and who I helped select clothes for a wedding he was attending.

17: ENTER PAUL NHS CONSULTANT

Six months went by since that strange encounter at M&S and then had an out-patients appointment at the Queen Elizabeth Hospital to have an x-ray and meet a consultant.

Initial meeting with nurse for preliminary checks, then sent for X-ray, came back to out-patients and was asked to wait in waiting area to see the duty consultant.

Surprise, surprise, as I entered the room it was the same guy, the one I helped with shopping at M&S. Can't say who was more pleased to see each other, him or me. One thing for sure it was a pleasant encounter, both beaming with big smiles.

We chatted; he told the nurse I was the one who helped choose his clothes for a family wedding he was attending

The Consultant, Paul, then proceeded to check my x-rays informing me nothing to worry about all was well but he would like to see me in six months' time for another check-up. I got up, thanking him and the nurse.

As I was about to walk out of the door, Paul called me back and passed a piece of paper to me with his personal phone number on. Not wanting to cause a scene, I slipped it into my handbag and saw him pass another piece of paper and pen. Assuming and not thinking, I quickly scribbled my mobile number on it. This happened right under the nurse's nose who was busy preparing for the next patient.

As I was leaving the consultation room, I turned round and smiled at him, and he smiled back at me.

This was another strange, unexpected encounter. As I walked towards the exit, I was in a trance could hardly believe what had just happened. I sensed a smile on my face and happiness beaming up from inside of me thinking what on earth just happened. Oh! Such joy and feeling of pure happiness. I felt like I was on cloud cuckoo land.

Later that evening, whilst I was watching the television, my mobile phone rang, reluctantly answering it as I had not recognised the number, I was surprised to hear

Paul's voice. We chatted about anything and everything and it seemed after a length of time when Paul suddenly asked, so when are we meeting. Lunch, dinner, you decide. I pretended to hesitate but was punching the air with excitement. Calming myself and my composure, I pretended to be busy for the next few days but sudden deep anxiety, sadness had overwhelmed me. This was most un-expected and since the Sanju's demise, I had never thought about going out with another person. Closed myself off to love and loving, the deep wounds inflicted by Sanju shut me off to that part of my life.

Paul was not taking no for an answer and after a lot of persuasion, I felt guilty for taking it out on him after all he was unaware of this tragic episode of my life. Reluctantly, I agreed to meet him for lunch.

(Lunch meeting with Paul)

Agreeing to meet up with Paul for lunch. Meet at The Swan Hotel Restaurant off the M5, Junction 16

On day of lunch feeling apprehensive as not sure why I had agreed to meet him.

Made effort to dress smart as on both previous occasions I was dressed casually, I mean joggers and sweatshirt with trainers. Nowadays, I am not inclined to dress smart and feel comfortable in casuals. Deep seated somewhere in my mind, I am deliberately warding off attracting attention. I have been known to dress elegantly and my ex-partner used to comment on how smart I looked and beautiful!! Since separating from him I have lost touch with that finesse I once had. So here I am dressed up in my casuals, jeans and t-shirt. Looking at myself in the mirror acknowledging my smartness but at the same time a feeling of sadness has overcome me. I sat down on my bed thinking that maybe I should cancel my lunch meeting with Paul. I can call him and make an excuse. I picked my mobile phone to call him then saw a missed call. I listened to his voice mail saying how much he was looking forward to our meeting and that he had already left the hospital for the day. Oh Bother! I felt trapped and duty bound to go convincing myself to enjoy a free lunch, assuming he was paying.

I got into my car having allowed enough time to get there including allowing for any delays on the motorway. Fortunately, there was no traffic and as I left the motorway, I could see the restaurant. I rolled into the car park conscious that I might be being watched. The car park was busy, I found a suitable spot and stepped out looking around to see if I could spot Paul but no sign of him. I walked towards the restaurant, entered the foyer and was immediately taken back at the business of the place. I stood there, looking round wondering which way to turn. Go to the bar order a drink or find somewhere to sit in case Paul hadn't arrived. Just then my thoughts were interrupted by someone tapping on my shoulder. I turned round to see Paul with outreached hand. I reached out to shake his hand, but he grabbed my hand leaning forward to plant a kiss on my cheek. We exchanged the usual niceties, how was your journey, did I find the place alright?

Paul guided me towards a table and as I was about to sit down, he looked at me and said that I looked beautiful almost unrecognisable. I was flattered, smiled at him and told him that he looked smart almost regretting having said it. He asked what I wanted to drink and walked off to the bar to get the drinks soon returning with them and a menu. I told him that I was surprised at his choice of restaurant as it was massive, very busy and open. He smiled and said that he wanted me to feel comfortable and not be pressured into assuming anything. How sweet of you, I thought to myself and decided to relax and let my guard down to enjoy. After chatting for a bit and perusing the menu, I let Paul know of my decision to order. He was surprised when I mention being a vegetarian. I am sure I saw him role his eyes, as he went off to order the meals. When he came back the topic turned to our personal lives. There wasn't much to tell him apart from having two grown up sons, my own property and a very big extended family. Paul mentioned that he did not have any children, that he had a villa in South of France he shared with his partner but interjected that their relationship had frittered out, more from his side and that he wanted her out, but she was dragging her feet. I must admit, I felt uncomfortable listening to him and wondering where this was leading. I did not have to wait long before he mentioned that he had passed his flying test and bought a Lancair 320, two-seat single-engine light aircraft. I congratulated him on passing his test and buying the two-seater plane. Thinking is this guy for real, a villa in South of France and now buying a light plane. I was already beginning to feel a bit lowly compared to his grand lifestyle. He said that he wanted me to be the first person to take a flight with him across the channel. Not what I expected, I went to pick my drink nearly dropping it as my hands were shaking. I started to look around the room expecting others to be eavesdropping on our conversation, but they all looked content with their conversations. I turned to look at him and said it was wonderful gesture on his part, but I will give it a miss and enjoy the meal saying that I am sure he will find some else to accompany him. The waiter interrupted us by asking who ordered what and placed my meal before me. Rest of the lunch was spent talking about various topics including the state of the country and being led by donkeys, he said it. After our meal, I asked to be excused to visit the ladies. When I came back, I noticed that he had changed his seating and as I walked up, he signalled for me to sit next to him. I pretended not to notice and sat on my usual seat. He commented something like, 'so is this how it's going to be?' I smiled and then laughed it off sensing Paul was looking and sounding different. I did not want to hang around and said that I needed to get back. He said that's a shame because I thought we could go somewhere comfortable adding that he had booked us a room and adding maybe he was pushing it a bit. Phew! I thought, my escape line. I was beginning to get a bit annoyed and wanted to escape fast, so I said that was true. I stood up and thanked him for the meal, shaking his hand. As I started walking out, he followed me saying least he could do was walk me to the car. Not a good idea, I thought and continued hastily walking away from him. He soon caught up with me and apologised for coming on strong, saying that he really likes me and wants to move things on. Not if I can help it!

I reached my car, went to open the door only to feel his presence close to me. I turned round to thank him. Paul was already too close to me, leaning forward to kiss me, but I turned my face with him kissing my cheek, again. I quickly got into my car waved to him and sped out of the car park without looking back. It was then I noticed I was shaking; I was angry and felt undermined. Who was I kidding thinking I was only coming out for lunch, with a stranger who I met twice briefly and once in capacity as a responsible consultant? I felt cheap, vulnerable, blaming myself for being such a fool, thinking I must have given the wrong signal. I was glad that I manged to get away given the pressure and talk of moving things on. All too sudden and unexpected, also realising that I had been away from the dating game a long time so not aware how things are done or expected to proceed. But it wasn't what I was expecting, the cheek of him booking a room for afters! Lucky escape.

I was glad to get home feeling safe as I shut my front door behind me. On hindsight, I realised there were various red flags during our conversation, somethings he said made me feel uncomfortable, uneasy but I chose to stick around and complete our lunch, maybe I should have left earlier. Overall, I felt silly!!

I realised that I was not ready for another relationship nor ever will be. Still feeling traumatised unable to trust anyone or let another person into my life. Better that way than pretend or ignore my feelings and emotions. I had paid a very heavy price wanting to appease Sanju, ignoring the warning signs.

Another (suitor), one bites the dust!

As I have variously questioned my own part, be it innocently, as a victim or ignoring the consequences of mine and other's actions, my thoughts turned to who or what had been driving my behaviours and tendencies. I have already mentioned my background and cultural upbringing but buried deep inside my consciousness and even sub-conscious was another element that was also, partly responsible for my behaviour: emotional, mental, spiritual and metaphysical.

So, bear with me as I tackle a part of me and many others that did have influence on me be it knowingly or un-willingly.

This I am going to address as the 'Spiritual and Intellectual minefields and teachings'. This required subtle research and admittance on my part that I was mis-lead, vulnerable in my desire to live and learn about self- development and enlightenment. Also to find answer to one of the age-old questions, 'Why are we here?'

15: SPIRITUAL & INTELLECTUAL MINEFIELDS TEACHINGS

(Survival, Sacrifices or Shambolic outcomes)

Classic belief was that only a few chosen ones can sacrifice their feelings or lives to help others on their journey. Years of reading personal development materials and wanting to be a good, kind-hearted person a cycle of Surviving Spiritual & Intellectual Minefields. My own thinking, beliefs had become 'so holier than thou', that I believed forgiveness was answer to all of life's problems including bad behaviours. That individuals walked own path and at any given time we were developed or at various levels of our beingness. Of course, the more I forgave, the better I felt thinking I was helping Sanju to grow and develop at his own pace and level. What a load of trollop all it did was give Sanju his 'get out of jail card' and dumping his problems into my lap making me responsible, not him, for his abusive behaviour. Thinking I could help him change by loving him and showing him consideration that he complained his family could not as they were all 'little people' with 'little minds' unlike me so superior and worldly almost putting me on a pedestal. Little did I know he was gaming me, had no intentions of changing. He was a wolf in sheep's clothing, always saying what needed to be said and full of praise for me, his soulmate hiding his true obnoxious nature.

All great thoughts have already been thought. What remains is to think them again.

You experience your own hidden genius / guru in the heart of another.

R W Emerson

More great words but what do they mean or how do they help with our day-to-day tussles in life? They don't! I can imagine myself sitting in one of these sessions whereby being one of, God knows, how many who haven't got a clue what is meant but won't raise their hand to ask for clarification due to risk of sounding stupid.

I have always been an ardent reader of spiritual and self-development books and seminars. Whilst attending a self-development seminar, I successfully did an eleven-foot Fire Walk, absolutely and as the saying goes,' been there, done it, got a T-Shirt', and still have it though never worn it. This experience has had a life changing effect on my life, all good, made me more self-confident and connected to myself but the downside was a belief that I needed to help others to achieve their potential(s).

During the last *three to four* decades there has been an explosion of Spiritual & Intellectuals who have taken on various shapes and forms to impress upon others their 'superior' knowledge and beingness. The knowledge and wisdom they sell is nothing more than information plagiarised from age old ethnic scriptures that have been revamped to make it sound authentic. Through changing words and in some instances creating a whole new language making it sound authentic work.

These so-called Self-help healers, masters, gurus, and/or their spiritual development materials, lay claims to improving lives. Why else would anyone invest their time or money?

As a normal, again I am doubting myself and what I mean by this statement, *human being*, I went in search of answers to myriads of questions about life and existence. To better myself, to feel I too belonged and was part of this existence, to go on a journey of self-discovery, self-development and self-identification or self-actualisation. Big, bold words used are not mine, but ones used to draw my interest to get me started on this journey. And so, I enrolled, paid money, attended seminars or read their dedicated material and waited for that change or any to happen. A point to note is that when I was reading their material or attending seminars there were immediate benefits realised. These benefits were not because of the causal change but my own desire to want to learn and to change. This was short lived because no sooner I put the book down or returned home from the seminar, I was back to square one living a normal life though in anticipation of something happening or changing that would/could make me feel better about myself or existing on a higher plane of self-consciousness.

My goal being enlightenment. That was the carrot and stick, the be all and end all that was promised.

Sadly, though after the event, there was no help or support available unless I was willing to invest more money or venture further into something else that may not be useful or related to original material. The so-called authors or presenters of the previous stuff have moved on to their next adventure to catch bigger, better audiences leaving behind even more troubled, unfulfilled souls, like me, struggling to bring normality back whilst still having expectations of bigger things to come. This set me on a path of finding out about the success of following other ideologies, religious or cultural?

Very quickly after some desk research and further book reading from spiritual leader, I came to the conclusions that there was no way of saying what the success rates were. As already stated, the aftermath of reading something new, seeing glowing reviews and falling into the trap of all is going to be well or being told if it isn't working, then have patience because human beings react differently to change and acceptance of it depending on their level of self-actualisation. Never mind us being fooled or batted away, the lies we tell ourselves to convince ourselves of that which is neither true nor vouched for apart from the book reviews or acknowledgements, and we know the reviews have been paid for or you scratch, my back and I your practices. That did not stop me from falling into the trap or being bamboozled by them (writers, gurus, masters and their written content). Some or most of them charlatans.

What happens when I read one of these self-development or spiritual books and needed some more information or help understanding it? Nothing! Nought!

There was no one available for me to turn to apart from joining the websites belonging of these so-called wonderful writers; masters, gurus, healers, ascended and chosen ones. On some of their websites, I came across claims about their greatness and counter claims about other's proclamations. However, if that was not bad enough, I was sign posted to paid membership with promises of getting personal lessons and on-line contact with them. These websites allude to the facts about divine success, positivity, all round improvements and gung-ho approaches. Informing me that thousands if not hundreds of thousands have been helped and pulled out of leading dire, miserable lives. It begged me to ask of myself.

What is wrong with me? Why am feeling low or worse than before I set on this journey of self-improvement/realisation? I needed to ask questions and get clarification from someone.

Up popped notification of another seminar or webinar asking me to join and send any questions prior to occasion. Unbelievable, it seems as if a divine miracle had occurred and my wishes to ask questions been answered. Being excited at the prospect of getting answers to my questions, I did exactly as request said and sent them in. I waited patiently for the big day when, hopefully, my questions will be answered. I was excited but instead of joining their webinar, I paid to attend in person. I travelled to London by train, took a taxi to the site and upon arrival filled in a form than was a handed a sticker with my name on it. I went into the seminar hall, found a seat, sat down and soon began chatting to persons on either side of me who were full of enthusiasm about the event. The seminar got off to the usual loud music, noises and introductions. I listened intently waiting for the questions and answers at the end of the session and soon names were mentioned, and the registered questions read out and duly answered. Some of the attendees raised their hands and got to ask their questions again cordially answered.

As the session was coming to an end and none of my questions had been mentioned, I raised my hand but was being ignored. Time was running out, so I stood up to attract attention but no chance and then came the announcement the session was ending and apologise for all who did not get their responses. It occurred to me all the questions asked and answered had been selected prior to the session and met the criteria of the meeting i.e., promoting this Guru or master's own philosophy. Mine were not selected and did not fit in with the general tone or momentum of the meeting. It occurred to me there and then, why would a negative question be answered especially one which starts with I am struggling to understand and need further clarification? That was not the purpose of this meeting, its purpose was to promote the presenter further and shine a light on the immense work that has been done to help mankind, accept me sitting there frustrated, feeling like shit, totally embarrassed thinking I had made a fool of myself sending in the questions expecting them to be answered. I was being asked to be part of charade, expected to be clapping, singing, waving my hands about and showing my excitement at being in the presence of this Guru or charlatan as that is how things started unfolding before my eyes. The whole evening had been stage managed, and chances are the question asked were pre-prepared. I left the venue hundreds of pounds poorer and none the wiser. on the way to the station, I bumped into one of the attendees who was equally disappointed and told me that he had attended such seminars before at different locations. He added that from his experience on the odd occasion when you raise your hand and do get to ask a question, you must be quick and accept the answer given, if not satisfied, you raise your hand again you either are ignored or attempts to shout loud enough to get heard, you will be admonished in front of the audience as a troublemaker and even told point blank that your question(s) has already been answered when they have not.

Above is another ruse, an attempt to use mind games to block attendees from asking legitimate questions and to convince them of their 'guru's' greatness, at the same time shielding his/their arrogance, allowing them to gain an upper hand over others and pretending him/her to be an almighty being, blessed by God to do his work on this earth.

Rubbish!

EGO is what most of these charlatans tend to relate to, convincing their followers to prostate before them, kiss their hand and lay precious gifts at their feet. Take for example this 'Cosmic Consciousness Guru' practicing or rather plagiarising material as his own, based in London. He claimed 'his life was changed by a spontaneous experience of 'cosmic consciousness at the age of sixteen', just before his spectacular fall from grace raising essential questions about the wider failings of the mythic guru tradition. Slowly but surely, to my own sense of being let down, being disappointed, I hesitatingly arrived at the conclusion that the history of spiritual communities is replete with stories of abuse and failure, and more than ever before the guru principle needs intense re-evaluation. As per my own experience, there must be lives ruined because there was no one to calm the storms created within their minds through either reading controversial materials, attending seminars, or belonging to cult organisations who all are well protected. These organisations have become money making machine or using their 'Guruship' status to fill their own pocket. These types of charlatans soon get found out. Why, because their greed gets better of them and sacrificing morals over moral high ground. I am also convinced that a true Guru does not need to try hard or push hard as nothing should matter as being in touch with one's own true beingness, not greatness or holiness.

In conclusion, nothing can take away from me the fact that when I needed spiritual guidance, I was either snubbed or made to feel subservient, hoping help would be provided to stop my mental torture, disturbances, being scared and fearful of my life given the demons running freely in my mind. This encounter had the potential to cause me more harm than good but remember whether Gurus or Pundits, I approached them because of their claim of being knowledgeable or enlightened, having wisdom and spiritual knowledge. All I came across turned out to be charlatan's, adept at hiding behind their own deceit and shortfalls. This encounter could have been dangerous and life threatening for me as I was already feeling vulnerable. Like many thousands, I set on this journey of finding the meaning of life without due thought of the dangers and innocence or ignorance thinking that Gurus or Pundits had the answers. Unfortunately, even if I was on a higher ground than them or needed guidance to achieve my potential, as far as these Gurus, Pundits, Masters are concerned, no one can be of any higher attainment than themselves. Therein lies the problem.

What started as doing a successful fire walk led me to free falling into obscurity. Though I am aware there must be, somewhere, genuine stoics and philosophers.

***************************The End **********************

Printed in Great Britain
by Amazon